Praise for
The *Love, California* Series
Empowering Romance with a Touch of Suspense

"A captivating world of glamour, romance, and intrigue."
— Melissa Foster, *New York Times* & *USA Today* Bestselling Author

"Jan Moran is the new queen of the epic romance."
— Rebecca Forster, *USA Today* Bestselling Author

"Jan rivals Danielle Steel at her romantic best.
— Allegra Jordan, author of *The End of Innocence*.

The Winemakers (St. Martin's Griffin)

"Beautifully layered and utterly compelling." — Jane Porter, *New York Times* & *USA Today* Bestselling Author

"Readers will devour this page-turner as the mystery and passions spin out." – *The Library Journal*

"Moran weaves knowledge of wine and winemaking into this intense family drama." – *Booklist*

Scent of Triumph (St. Martin's Griffin)

"A sweeping saga of one woman's journey through WWII. A heartbreaking, evocative read!"
— Anita Hughes, Author of *Lake Como*

"A dedicated look into world of fashion; recommend<
— *Midwest B*

D0517563

Sparkle

A Love, California Novel

Book Number 6

by

Jan Moran

SUNNY PALMS

PRESS

Library of Congress Cataloging-in-Publication Data
Moran, Jan.
/ by Jan Moran
ISBN 978-1-942073-93-2 (softcover)
ISBN 978-1-942073-91-8 (ebooks)

Printed in the U.S.A.
Cover design by Ginna Moran
Cover images copyright 123RF
For Inquiries Contact: Sunny Palms Press
9663 Santa Monica Blvd STE 1158
Beverly Hills, CA, USA
www.SunnyPalmsPress.com, www.JanMoran.com

Books by Jan Moran

Contemporary
The Love, California Series:
Flawless
Beauty Mark
Runway
Essence
Style
Sparkle

20th Century Historical
The Winemakers: A Novel of Wine and Secrets
Scent of Triumph: A Novel of Perfume and Passion
Life is a Cabernet: A Companion Wine Novella to The Winemakers

Nonfiction
Vintage Perfumes

To hear about Jan's new books first and get special offers, join Jan's VIP Readers Club at www.JanMoran.com and download a free read.

1

Beverly Hills, California

"MORE CHAMPAGNE, MISS?"

Elena Eaton accepted a glass of sparkling bubbly from a server. Veuve Clicquot, she noted, wanting to remember everything about this night. For a girl who'd grown up surfing the waves of Bondi Beach in Sydney, Australia, she never thought she'd be standing in the middle of the brightest stars in Hollywood, mingling and eating caviar at an Academy Awards after-party as if it were what she did every day of her life.

Among the crowd of actors, directors, and producers, little gold statuettes glittered—and yes, they really were much heavier than they looked, she noted—cradled in the arms of the lucky winners who could now command much more per film as an Oscar winner. Most winners had passed the statuettes off to trusted assistants, while a few refused to be parted from their new acquisition.

"Are you enjoying yourself?" asked Aimee Winterhaus, the editor of *Fashion News Daily* in New York and the host and underwriter of the party.

"I'm thrilled to be here, Aimee."

When the industry insider had asked their friend Penelope where the hottest new place in Los Angeles was to host a private after-party, she had told Aimee about Bow-Tie, owned by her friends Lance Martel and Johnny Silva. The restaurant was in one of a handful of old houses that had been converted to business use on the busy shopping street.

Aimee had hired an event company, and now the entire place looked like a 1920s speakeasy with casino tables, velvet drapes, and glamorous images of Golden Age stars projected on the walls. Not to mention the life-sized ice sculpture of the Oscar statuette. Some A-list actors were gathered at the bar, but many were in a private VIP dining room across from what Elena guessed had once been a large living room. She loved the hardwood floors and the brick fireplaces that anchored the rooms.

"I can't stop looking at everyone," Elena said. "The gowns, the jewelry—"

"The hot actors," Aimee added with a sly smile.

Elena grinned. "Very hot actors." Aimee was right. Her friends in Sydney were going nuts over this. Allison, her best friend from school, had even organized a viewing party at the bed-and-breakfast she owned with her husband Zach.

"You could meet someone tonight," Aimee said, raising

a perfectly arched eyebrow. "The night's young."

"I'm hardly their type," Elena said, twisting her glossy, nude-colored lips to one side. She'd shimmied into a sleek black halter dress that skimmed her hips and fell to the floor, though she felt more comfortable in yoga pants sitting crossed-legged with her sketch pad. Or concentrating at her work bench surrounded by jewelry-making tools. "I'm only glam on the outside tonight."

"Glam is as glam does," Aimee said, laughing. "Trust me, with the right makeup and clothes, we make fourteen-year-old models look like movie stars."

Penelope and Fianna had tried to talk her into a sizzling red dress, but she was so nervous tonight that the last thing she wanted was to stand out in the crowd. Besides, the black velvet showcased the delicate blue diamond necklace and earrings she'd just designed to match her deep blue eyes. And black was slimming, of course. Although she was comfortable in her skin, next to uber-fit celebrities she needed any help she could get.

She touched the stone in her necklace for luck.

Most everyone in the industry tonight had turned out to laud their fellow casts and crews and the night was just beginning. Most people would glide from one party to another—to the *Vanity Fair* party, the Governors Ball, and parties hosted by Lionsgate, Women in Film, and other producers and organizations.

Every event was over-the-top designed; she'd never been

to parties like these. Her social life usually involved campfires on the beach, or binge-watching a new TV series with friends. Elena was so excited to be trailing her friend Penelope—a top fashion model—wherever she went.

Equally impressive were the jewels that sparkled on svelte throats, dainty earlobes, and slender wrists and fingers of well-known actresses. Some even wore hundreds of thousands of dollars of gemstones in their hair.

Everywhere Elena looked were shimmering diamonds, emeralds, rubies, and sapphires. Even deep purplish-blue tourmalines. Estimating values, she figured many stars wore jewelry valued at millions of dollars.

So did Penelope.

Elena pressed her hand against her fluttering heart to calm her anxiety. She had pledged her entire business against the jewelry she'd designed for Penelope to wear tonight. Which was why she'd hardly let her friend out of her sight all evening.

She caught Penelope's glance and wiggled her fingers in a tiny wave. Penelope lit up and made her way across the room. Watching her, Elena admired how Penelope moved and showcased her jewelry and dress to perfection. She watched heads turn in Penelope's wake, and heard murmurs of approval trailing her as she passed.

Penelope looked like a glittery mermaid princess who'd just emerged from the sea. She'd even changed her hair color from purple to blond with turquoise and azure highlights to go with the stunning aqua silk gown she wore, which was designed by another friend of theirs, Fianna Fitzgerald.

The blazing marine blue and twinkling green diamonds at Penelope's throat were worth a fortune and had drained Elena of her personal gemstone coffers—not to mention the cost of additional stones, other materials, and her labor.

Inspired by opulent jewelry from India, she'd spent months designing the suite that included earrings, bracelets, and rings, but the piece she was most proud of was the lacy, cascading choker with diamonds arranged in a wave-like pattern from light to dark.

Most important to her was the lineage of these fancy-colored diamonds, and what they represented to her family. She'd never shared the true provenance of these stones with anyone outside her family, not even her closest friends. Nor *could* she. In her heart, they would always be Sabeena's diamonds. And in her ancestor's honor, she had marked a large part of their profit on sale for a special cause.

"Elena." Penelope gripped Elena's hands and said hello to Aimee. "Your jewelry and Fianna's dress outshine me tonight," she said, laughing. "They're the real stars."

"You're not a top model for nothing," Aimee said, reaching out to touch the lacy bejeweled choker that Elena had designed. "Those are exquisite fancy-colored diamonds."

"Thanks for wearing them, Penelope," Elena said, in awe of how beautiful Penelope looked tonight. She knew her as a friend, just a regular person she traveled with—most recently when Penelope had come under threat from a deranged psychotic fan by the name of Kristo.

"It's the least I can do," Penelope said, her tawny eyes brimming with elation. "You helped me get through a tough time."

"It turned out well though," Elena said. "How's the new show going?"

Penelope's face shone with excitement. "We started filming, and I'm working on ideas for more episodes. The next one will be Denmark. Isn't that exciting? I'll get to see my parents then."

"Hey hottie, how about more bubbly?"

A familiar voice rang out beside Elena. She turned, widening her eyes in surprise at the sight of an old boyfriend from Sydney, the older brother of her friend Allison. "Shane? What are you doing here?"

"Following the waves." He handed Aimee a fresh glass. "Making my way toward Maui and picking up work along the way." He tapped Elena's nose. "That's new," he said, indicating the tiny, blue diamond nose-stud glinting on her left nostril.

She ignored his comment; he'd lost his right to comment on her years ago. "You're not working at Bow-Tie regularly are you?" This was her favorite restaurant, and she'd die if she had to see him here all the time.

"Just the big party," he replied with a wink at her. Turning to Penelope, he said, "That's quite the jewelry you're wearing. Big rocks, there." He let his eyes slide over Penelope.

"Keep your eyes and your hands to yourself." Elena wanted to slap the floppy blond hair right out of his eyes. Tan and buff, he was a surfer dude out for fun. And faithful to no woman. His sister couldn't be more different.

Penelope laughed off his remark with grace. "You're a friend of Elena's? These are her designs."

"Not a friend," Elena said, scolding him with narrowed eyes.

Ignoring her expression, Shane gave her a smooth grin. "Nice work, Elena. Taking a step up in the world, are you?"

"Don't you have work to do?" The last thing she needed tonight was Shane hovering around. She was on edge enough as it was. Though he was good-looking, no way would she fall for his tricks again.

Shane wagged his brows and sailed through the crowd, stopping to flirt with every attractive woman.

"Good riddance," Elena muttered.

Aimee looked at her with amusement. "Don't let him get to you."

"I won't," Elena said, flipping her hair from her forehead. She had more to worry about than Shane.

"As for the new nose bling, I love it," Penelope said.

Aimee nodded. "Very sexy. Accents your eyes."

"I've got to run, too," Penelope said. "My producer wants me to meet some people." She smiled. "But I'm posing for every picture I can for you and Fianna."

"Lovely to see you shining so brightly after that awful mess, Penelope." Aimee leaned in to air kiss the model goodbye.

Nervous didn't even begin to describe how Elena felt. Terrified was more like it. Yet the exposure from tonight and an important jewelry sale could elevate her struggling business into the stratosphere, secure her family, and more. She hoped an offer for her work would come in after photos circulated.

"Just look at that Chanel. Simply sublime." Aimee waved and nodded at several attendees she knew. "Besides the Met Gala in New York and the Cannes Film Festival, this is the best place to photograph stars in the most beautiful attire."

"And jewelry," Elena said, glancing around in appreciation.

Aimee ticked off her fingers. "The European designers are out in force. I've seen Chanel, Dior, Armani Privé, Valentino, Louis Vuitton, Gucci, and Givenchy. And the Americans are here with Carolina Herrera, Monique Lhuillier, Ralph Lauren, and Lele Rose."

Taking a breath, Elena asked, "Which outfit do you like best?"

"I'd have to say Penelope's. Fianna has a fresh, new point of view."

Elena gazed at the fluid, aqua silk dress Penelope wore that Fianna had fit to her. She also admired how Penelope wore the diamond set—the *parure*—she'd designed.

In rare fancy colors ranging from deep vivid blue to greyish blue, from sea foam green to forest shades—colors rivaling the legendry Hope and Dresden Green diamonds—the stones were set in platinum that glittered against Penelope's glowing skin. The delicate choker rose high on her neck and draped across her collarbone, dipping to her décolletage.

This was her masterpiece, simply the finest work she'd ever done.

Her heart quickened at the brilliance of the natural stones, faceted to perfection, framing Penelope's long, graceful neck. Jewelry design was Elena's artistic expression. She loved the luminosity of gemstones, the precision work of design, and the sheer beauty of creation.

The patina of history burnished the world's most famous gemstones, adding luster to remarkable stones. From the whispered curses of the magnificent Koh-i-Noor and Black Orlov diamonds, to the incredible Star of India—a star sapphire the size of a golf ball—to the heart-shaped Taj Mahal Diamond that Richard Burton had bought for Elizabeth Taylor. As well the La Peregrina Pearl that Taylor's beloved dog almost swallowed. Elena loved all the stories.

Her gemstones had their own secret history, too. And now was their time.

For months, she and Fianna had worked together to create the most visually stunning, coordinated ensemble on the red carpet for Penelope. They had neighboring shops on Robertson Boulevard and often worked long into the night together. If Penelope's photographs were chosen as fashion magazine leads, their countless hours of hard work and huge financial gambles would pay off.

Smiling with satisfaction, Elena saw another person admiring the choker on Penelope. She couldn't have asked for a more perfect model and showcase for taking her jewelry line to the next level, so she'd invested everything she had—and could borrow—into it.

"Penelope looks perfect tonight," Elena said. "Wouldn't she make a great cover?"

"Absolutely." Aimee smoothed her sleek black bob and held a finger to her red lips. "As a matter of fact, Penelope *will* be our cover next week. You should see the red carpet photography we got. And your jewelry is dazzling. Get ready to write orders, darling. Your pieces are bound to be snapped up by some billionaire."

Elena was so excited she bear-hugged Aimee, the imperious industry editor many designers were nearly afraid of. "I'm so excited, thank you!" She fervently hoped her work would be sold. She had been knocking on retailer doors for years with limited success. Either she hadn't had a big enough name, or she couldn't produce the volume they needed.

Elena had been saving her money a long time for this expensive wager. So when Penelope had offered to wear her designs—and Fianna's—both women jumped at the chance.

Elena had known that only diamonds would do. She glanced around. Fianna was somewhere in the crowd, mingling and having a great time.

Aimee moved on to greet another winner just as Elena's phone buzzed in her purse. A text message popped up on her screen from her cousin Coral in San Diego. *OMG! The entire Bay family watched the Academy Awards. Saw Penelope Plessen on the red carpet. Jewels are AMAZING!*

Elena smiled at her cousin's message. Her mother, Honey, had grown up in San Diego. Elena had loads of aunts, uncles, and cousins in the area. *Too many Bays on that shore,* her dad often said. She loved his corny jokes, and that's where she'd gotten her sassy mouth, her mother claimed.

Just then another text appeared from Coral's sister, Poppy, a journalism student who was handling her publicity. *Get photos!*

Elena grinned. She couldn't wait to tell Poppy about Aimee and the *Fashion News Daily* cover.

As she texted her cousins, Elena kept an eye on Penelope. Her boyfriend Stefan, who owned a bodyguard service for the rich and famous, kept close to her. Still, she was anxious every time she thought about the fortune around Penelope's neck. She couldn't help but think what might happen. Every possible disaster had crossed her mind.

"Hey, why the frown?" Fianna appeared next to her, her long red hair framing her face in loose curls.

"It's just my imagination running bonkers again." Elena

gave an unsteady laugh.

Fianna nodded toward Shane. "He's sexy. Saw you talking to him. Someone you know?"

"Someone I never wanted to see again. I dated him in Sydney when we were teenagers." She shuddered. "First kiss." Changing the subject, Elena said, "Penelope is such a professional. Look at how she moves in your dress."

"This is more than I dared to dream about." Fianna let out a little squeak of excitement.

Elena nudged her and winked. "Can you believe this is happening?"

"I need lots of pictures. I might never make it here again." Fianna gripped Elena's hand with excitement. "I met a costume designer who was gushing over Penelope's dress. Did you see her?" Not waiting for an answer, Fianna glanced at her. "Looks like you have a real problem. Your champagne glass is empty and you need dessert. Come with me."

Elena hesitated, not wanting to let Penelope out of her sight. "Bring me something?"

"You can't stare at Penelope all night. We need to meet other celebrities, too. There's a lot of potential business here."

With reluctance, Elena acquiesced. "You're right."

Fianna took her hand and led her toward a table laden with delectable treats that Lance and his kitchen staff had made. Exquisite miniature fruit tarts, tiny crème brûlée, chocolate mousse, gold foiled statuettes. "Yum," Fianna said, picking up a plate.

Glancing back, Elena saw Stefan excuse himself from Penelope, motion toward another one of his bodyguards who was also in attendance for another star, and walk toward them. He looked handsome in an ebony tuxedo that showed off his broad shoulders and trim waist. Elena was happy for Penelope that she'd reconnected with the love of her life.

Stefan slowed by them. "Having fun, ladies?"

"Best time ever," Fianna said.

"I'm still pinching myself," Elena added. "Penelope is a vision."

"Isn't she?" Stefan gazed after her, admiration evident in his eyes.

Elena traded a look with Fianna, and they both released a little sigh. With all the gorgeous women in the room, Stefan's heartstrings were firmly tied to Penelope. And they had nearly missed the chance to reconnect.

She had never dated a man who looked at her the way Stefan looked at Penelope. The surfers she'd dated in Sydney and San Diego only wanted big waves and good times.

Drawing a shaky breath, Elena leaned toward Stefan. "I'm jittery just watching Penelope. My entire net worth and everything I could borrow is hanging on her neck and earlobes."

"Relax, Elena, we've got this." Stefan winked and moved on toward the restrooms.

She certainly hoped so. When she was young, she'd started making jewelry as a sideline to support her surfing habit but soon became more enamored with designing new pieces than chasing waves. After saving her money, she'd traveled to the San Diego area to study at the Gemological Institute of America—the GIA—in Carlsbad where she honed her skills in gemology and jewelry design. She'd worked hard to become a world-class designer, and now, here she was on the brink of success. She hoped.

"Don't look so stressed," Fianna said. "Think of all the opportunities here."

Elena caught her breath again, hardly believing this night was real. By the time tonight's photos hit social media, newspapers, and magazines, her world could change.

She couldn't let her parents down either. They'd invested their savings in her vision, too. She shouldn't bypass any chance before her. "Guess we better circulate."

"We might as well indulge first," Fianna said, selecting a raspberry tart. "We don't have to worry about being photographed like the stars."

Elena eyed a trio of chocolate delights. "This is why I work out." She chose a miniature dark chocolate sculpture of a movie reel decorated with sea salt and raspberries.

"Hey you two."

Turning around, Elena's frown dissolved into a wide smile at three women who'd just joined them. Exchanging air kisses and hugs, she greeted her friends. That afternoon, Fianna had closed her boutique and they'd all gathered there to get dressed and made up.

Penelope had brought in hair stylists and makeup artists from High Gloss, and Fianna had her alterations staff there to help her clients and friends choose dresses from her racks and make any last minute adjustments. They'd blasted music and everyone had been in such high spirits. Lance and Johnny from Bow-Tie had sent salads and sandwiches, which Elena had been too nervous to eat.

Elena was so glad they were all together sharing this special night. Verena and Scarlett were dating the partners at Bow-Tie, Lance and Johnny, so they'd been able to get in. As for Dahlia, her grandmother Camille knew all the celebrities from years ago to the present. "How'd it go at the High Gloss station?"

"It was so exciting to talk to all the stars," Verena said. She was wearing a royal blue one-shoulder dress that reflected her eyes, and her pale blond hair curved around her face. "Many of them were nervous, so we found ourselves calming them." She turned to Fianna. "And everyone loved our dresses. They all know your name now."

Penelope had suggested to High Gloss Cosmetics CEO Olga Kaminsky that she bring in Verena and Dahlia to provide skincare and perfume to accompany the High Gloss color line at backstage makeup stations at the awards. Artists were providing touchups for the stars before they went on stage. Between tears and perspiration, some of the actors were a mess.

"I got so many selfies," Dahlia said. "Can you believe

it—the *stars* were suggesting it." She looked stunning in a strapless, emerald green dress, along with earrings to match that Elena had custom designed for her a couple of years ago. Dahlia's grandmother Camille had commissioned the earrings as a birthday surprise.

"That's because they found out she's dating Alain Delamare and a lot of them are Formula 1 fans." Scarlett tapped Verena on the shoulder and laughed.

"I hardly said a word," Verena replied. "People recognized Dahlia from that finish line kiss in Monaco that was blasted around the world. They kept saying, 'haven't I seen you somewhere before?'" Her lip curved in a mischievous smile. "I just helped them remember."

As they talked and laughed, Elena continued to glance at Penelope. Guests moved between them as the party went on. She didn't see Stefan, and she began to wonder what was keeping him, though she knew he had other clients there, too, as well as other bodyguards on staff discreetly standing by.

Scarlett noticed her unease. "Relax, Elena."

"There are so many people." Of all her friends, Scarlett, her business attorney, knew exactly what was at stake.

While her friends talked, Elena searched the crowd, watching Penelope again as she moved from one group to another. Her vision was blocked by a tall, thirty-something guy in a tuxedo. With glossy black hair and a trimmed shadow of a beard, he turned and caught her trying to peer past him.

She couldn't be sure, but she thought Penelope might have disappeared into the private VIP room.

"Looking for someone?" His brow furrowed as if she'd interrupted him.

Elena stepped aside and looked past him. "I'm good."

"Maybe. But that's not what I asked."

"Excuse me?" She'd just dealt with Shane and didn't need another inconsiderate oaf to spoil her evening. Not that neither of them could.

He stepped into her line of sight. "Are you here alone?"

Elena put a hand on her hip. "If that's a pick-up line, you'll have to do better than that, mate." She blinked. *Was that the champagne talking?* He was nice-looking, if you liked that sort of brooding thing. Which she didn't.

His eyes slid down her neck, and the crease between his dark brows deepened. "I'm Jake."

Where *was* Penelope? She'd lost sight of her.

"And you are?"

"Definitely looking for someone else." Elena fidgeted with her necklace, sliding her fingers over it as if to protect it from his view.

"Actress?"

"Excuse me." She stepped to one side, but a passerby bumped her back into the man of a hundred questions and she toppled off her high heels, sloshing champagne on his shirt. "Oh, bugger—"

"Got you." He steadied her.

"Sorry." She dabbed his shirt with her napkin. She couldn't help but notice that he was pretty firm under there. Probably spent his days working out. A bar bouncer, if she had to guess. Or actor, she corrected herself, remembering where she was.

He caught her hand. "It's okay."

He plucked the crumpled napkin from her hand.

"Jason, I'll get another—"

"Jake." Shaking his head, he stepped to a nearby table and grabbed a cloth napkin. "Actresses," he muttered.

"I heard that. What makes you think I'm an actress, and what's wrong with that?" She knew a lot of working actors—women and men—and they were dedicated to their craft. Some became big stars, but for most of them, it required discipline to maintain a modest living doing what they loved.

Jake swung around. "First, you're pretty in a glossy sort of way, second, you were talking to Penelope Plessen and Aimee Winterhaus—though you're not thin enough to be a model—and third, that's definitely not your own jewelry."

Elena's lips parted in astonishment. *How presumptuous.* "Look, mate, I'll have you know—"

Suddenly, the closed door to the VIP room flung open and screams erupted, piercing the music that throbbed above the incessant chatter. Some of the biggest celebrities flooded from the room, tumbling over each other to get out.

A woman stumbled out in shock. "We've been robbed!"

In the commotion, the woman next to Elena stepped on

her hemline. Her heel caught in the fabric and jerked Elena down hard, pinning her to her spot.

"Damn it," Jake exclaimed, just as Elena flailed backward. His strong arms wrapped around her, keeping her upright, but his attention was riveted across the restaurant.

"Where's Penelope?" Every worry she'd had suddenly surged to the surface.

"Stay here," Jake said, yanking her skirt free and leaving her. He cut through the pandemonium toward the VIP room.

"There she is," Fianna said, pointing across the room.

Elena stood on her tip-toes to see past the throngs of people scurrying about. "Oh no…"

Across the room, Penelope had emerged from the VIP room, where other stars were also looking frightened and dazed. Her hands were clasped around her bare throat.

Her necklace was gone.

Elena cried out in anguish and pushed toward Penelope, who sank to her knees on the floor, her head in her hands, now bare of the stunning ring and bracelet that Elena had created. From the corner of her eye, she saw Stefan racing toward her with Jake not far behind.

"Penelope!" Elena cried out, her heart pounding as she watched Penelope go limp in Stefan's arms. She'd only taken her eyes from her for a minute. Oh, why hadn't she insisted on staying with her?

She'd never forgive herself if her friend had been hurt.

2

"PENELOPE!" ELENA'S NERVES jangled her sanity as she cut through the horrified crowd pressing forward. She'd seen her friend in action—Penelope did a martial arts workout and had taken care of herself before.

So what had happened?

"I'm right behind you," Scarlett said, lifting the hem of her coral sequined dress.

"Oh, my God," Fianna cried, hurrying with them. "I knew it would be a night to remember, but I never dreamed it would end like this."

"Everyone stay where you are." Stefan bounded toward the door, immediately seizing control of the situation to make sure those inside were safe. Lifting Penelope to her feet, he made sure she was unharmed. Once satisfied, he cordoned off the area. "You're witnesses, so no one leaves this room," he said, raising his voice to those remaining in the VIP room before racing toward the rear entry of Bow-Tie.

Jake charged ahead of him and both men pushed past

Shane, who stood nearby looking shocked and helpless.

"For God's sake, help them," Elena yelled at Shane. He was as useless as always.

Guards poured inside from their posts at the front of the restaurant. All around them, guests gestured and exclaimed.

"Excuse me, pardon me." As Elena continued to work her way through the teaming crowd, she caught snippets of conversation. *Robbery…jewelry stolen…escaped…* Elena clenched her teeth.

Standing on her tiptoes, she motioned toward Penelope, who now leaned against the doorway to the dining area heaving deep breaths. When she finally reached Penelope, she threw her arms around her grief-stricken friend.

Penelope pressed her hand against her bare neck. "Oh, Elena, I'm so sorry." Tears spilled from her eyes, and her words tumbled out. "Three men dressed like waiters. With guns. They blocked the room. Stripped us of our jewelry and valuables so fast, then ran out the back." She drew her shaky fingers over her barren earlobes and neck. "It was horrible…"

Elena hugged her. "Thank God you're okay. That's all that matters," she said. She meant it, though her heart was breaking.

Scarlett went inside the VIP room and they followed her. She walked toward the rear door. "Bet they left that behind." With the pointy tip of her gold shoe, she pointed toward a metal device of some sort that lay on the hearth near the exit. "That could be evidence. We need to leave everything just as it is for the police."

"How awful," Elena said, quivering inside. "Was anyone else hurt?"

"Just Cody." Penelope nodded toward an actor who'd won the Best Supporting Actor award tonight. He pressed a white handkerchief over a bloody cut above his eye. "He tried to go Rambo on one of the guys and got whacked with a gun. Lucky he wasn't killed."

Just then, Penelope's phone rang. Frowning, she pulled it from her purse. "Hi Dad. I'm okay, but how did you know?" She shot a look toward Elena. "I was robbed, too."

While Penelope talked to her father, Elena comforted an older woman next to her who looked like she was going to pass out. Scarlett was aiding another person, and she'd asked her boyfriend Johnny to bring trays of water—or whatever the people wanted—for the guests while they waited. Security guards were asking people not to leave.

The entire restaurant was in a state of turmoil with people anxious to make sure friends were unharmed, others wailing over their losses, and still others furiously tapping their phones to check in with family.

"I've got to post this to social media," the young woman next to her said, holding her phone above the crowd to capture the chaos.

Anxiously, Johnny leaned toward Scarlett. "The police should be here shortly. Can you help?"

Scarlett gripped his hands and kissed him on the cheek.

"Of course I will."

Johnny tugged his bow-tie. "Our first awards after-party, and this is what happens. We did everything we could think of to make sure guests would be safe." He turned to Elena and gave her a hug. "How are you doing?"

Elena couldn't find the words. *How am I doing now that everything I invested—and borrowed—has been snatched from Penelope?*

Scarlett touched Elena's shoulder. "The robbers got the jewelry she'd designed for Penelope."

"*Ay, Dios mío.*" Johnny looked crestfallen. "Surely they'll catch who did this."

"The police are going to have their hands full." Penelope put her phone back into her purse. "My dad was on Twitter looking at all the photos when the hashtag erupted. Someone is live-tweeting from here."

Jake stepped back into the VIP room, huffing from the exertion of the chase.

"See anything?" Johnny asked.

His hands on his hips, Jake shook his head. "They worked fast. Those were pros." He cast his gaze around the room, and when he saw Elena, he frowned. "You weren't in here when it happened. You need to leave now." He caught her hand and started toward the VIP entryway.

"Neither were you. Let go of me," she snapped, pulling her hand free. *Who was this guy?*

"We need to secure the area."

"These are my friends and I'm not going anywhere."

Stefan appeared behind her. "She's with us, Jake."

Elena swung around. "You know this jerk?"

Stefan nodded. "Jake's in insurance."

"Like auto, home, and fire?" Elena asked with sarcasm.

"Yeah," Jake said, curling his lip in derision. "As long as it's a Ferrari or a multi-million dollar estate."

"You're beyond rude," Elena rolled her eyes and stalked back to Penelope and Scarlett.

Jake swept a chair into each hand and followed her. When he reached Penelope, he placed one beside her and said, "In case you want to rest your feet from those stunning shoes." Indicating to Scarlett, he added, "And one for you."

"Why, thank you." Penelope sank onto the chair.

He threw a swift look at Elena. "See how rude I am?"

"Where's mine?" Elena shot back.

"Manners," he said. A corner of his mouth turned up.

Scarlett perched on the edge and patted hers. "We can share."

When Elena remained standing, her arms folded across her chest, Scarlett tugged the skirt of her dress. "It's going to be a long night."

"If he's around, it sure will be." Elena plopped down beside her friends.

"At least he's easy on the eyes," Scarlett said, watching Jake taking charge to settle the crowd.

"Stefan's got a lot of nice friends," Penelope said.

Elena huffed. "You're biased." The last thing she needed right now was a guy with an attitude. It was all she could do to keep from crying. She bit her lip, blinking hard.

Reaching for her hand, Penelope said, "If I'd ever dreamed this might happen, I wouldn't have worn your jewelry. I feel awful." She squeezed her hand. "I'll make it up to you."

"You don't have to do that. I knew the risk."

Stefan returned and handed Penelope a glass. "Thought you could use a cranberry juice to keep your energy up. Jake's bringing more for you two."

Pulling out her phone, Scarlett began tapping notes. "Penelope, who's your insurer?"

"Greyson International."

"You're in luck," Stefan said. "Jake's dad started Greyson."

Scarlett added the information. "How do you know him?"

"When I was practicing law at the firm," Stefan began, "Jake was once an expert witness for me. He's an investigator who specializes in fraud detection. The expensive kind. My client's husband had faked a theft of her jewelry. Before he began to poison her."

"Oh, no. Then what happened?" Penelope asked.

Stefan shrugged. "She shot him. She was up on charges of premeditated murder, but we got her off. She'd had replicas of her best pieces made for travel, but her new husband didn't know that. He stole the wrong pieces. So we proved she didn't care about the jewels."

Drawn into the story, Elena asked, "Then why'd she shoot him?"

A deep voice floated behind her. "Because he was rude to her."

Elena whirled around to see Jake standing behind her. "Why, you—"

"Cranberry juice?" Jake handed a beverage to Scarlett, who gratefully accepted it.

"You know what you can do with that," Elena said, crossing her arms.

"Cheers." Jake drank it down in a long gulp.

Fury gathered in her chest, and she felt her cheeks flush with heat. How dare this man make fun of her now on the worst night of her life, after she'd just lost everything she'd gambled? She rose and jabbed him in the chest. "You're disgusting."

Unable to contain her emotions any longer, she pushed past him and fled to the ladies room. There in the crowded bathroom, not caring who else was there, she leaned against the wall and broke down, tears spilling onto her cheeks. She was beyond embarrassed. How would she tell her parents? *I'll gladly bet on your horse*, her dad had told her as he wrote a check, pitching in a large chunk of their savings to fund her effort.

She'd have to call them, she realized, and a fresh sob

seized her. She reached out, fumbling for a paper towel.

"Let me help you." An older actress she recognized, Barbara Charles, pulled out a paper towel, wet it, and pressed it against Elena's hot face as she gulped for air. Beneath immaculate, highlighted blonde hair, ruby and diamond earrings illuminated the older woman's Technicolor green eyes. "There, there," she murmured, gently turning Elena away from others in the room. "Now that's a worthy performance," she said, kindness in her voice. "Are you an actor?"

Elena smiled through quivering lips, grateful for the company. "Jeweler. Penelope Plessen is—*was*—wearing pieces I designed." The reality of the night hit her again, and she choked back a moan.

"I'm so sorry for you," Barbara said. "I saw Penelope earlier, and she looked gorgeous. That necklace…utterly remarkable. You're really quite talented, aren't you? And determined to have gotten this far." Without waiting for a reply, she fished a pressed linen handkerchief from her purse and then paused, inclining her head. "Do we know each other?"

Elena shook her head. She'd seen the actress once at a fundraiser she'd attended for a shelter for abused women, where she often volunteered, but they'd never met.

"I don't forget faces like yours." Barbara touched her handkerchief to Elena's forehead.

"Shelter Haven Home. I volunteer."

"That's it." She looked toward the door. "The police arrived just as I came in. You'll have to talk to them, so take a moment and pull yourself together." Pressing the monogrammed linen square into Elena's hand, she added, "Careful with your makeup."

Despite the living nightmare, Elena nodded and tried to catch her breath.

"That's it. Chin up," Barbara said, running a manicured finger under Elena's jawline. "Now go out there and make sure they get your jewelry back for you."

Elena dabbed her eyes and handed the handkerchief back to Barbara. "Thanks. I'm so embarrassed." The actress had played a lot a feisty characters in films, but she seemed thoughtful and genuine.

"Keep it," Barbara said. "I brought extras for tonight." She offered her arm to Elena. "Let's go show everyone what we're made of."

Another woman held the door for them, and Elena tried not to clutch Barbara's arm as tightly as she really wanted to.

As directed, Elena dried her eyes, lifted her chin, and swished into the restaurant, her arm linked with that of one of Hollywood's most beloved actresses. She still wanted to die inside, but Barbara's insistence gave her strength.

"Always make an entrance," Barbara whispered.

All at once, Elena halted at the familiar sight of a broad-shouldered man.

As Jake turned and saw her, the smile slipped from his

face. "What are you doing with my mom?"

Before Elena could answer, Barbara replied, "Don't be so rude. What have I told you about that?" To Elena, she said, "Pardon my son, he's forgotten his manners.'

3

THROUGHOUT HIS LIFE, Jake had been constantly amazed at the people his mother knew and had forgotten to tell him about. *It's part of the job,* she'd say. *I meet everyone, darling.*

But how the hell did she know this one? He didn't even know the girl's name, he realized.

"Your son?" A smile played on those full, glossy lips of hers. "He *has* forgotten his manners," the younger woman replied, looking haughty.

His mother patted her arm conspiratorially. "Jake never learned the *savoir faire* necessary for Hollywood. He's in insurance. Like my late husband."

"I know a lot more than you give me credit for, Mom," Jake said, offering his arm to his mother, but never taking his eyes from the ravishing creature on her other arm. Annoying is what she was, with that short, sassy brown hair. With the most incredible earrings that dusted her exquisite neck. Dazzling stones suspended from a long platinum thread. And that necklace…

He peered closer. Not sapphire, not tanzanite. They had remarkable depth and fiery brilliance. If he were to guess, those stones looked like rare blue diamonds. If they were—and if they were genuine—they were probably bought for her by some unsuspecting billionaire geek. He had to know.

Jake nodded toward her necklace nestled in the hollow of her neck. "A blue diamond?"

Her glossy lips parted in surprise. She slid her fingers over it, dipping her head slightly.

Before he received a reply, his mother slipped her hand onto his crooked arm and tilted her head toward the younger woman. "He's my date."

Jake noticed a discreet flower tattoo just behind the young woman's ear. And a nose-stud. His curiosity piqued, he wondered about her. However, answers would have to wait.

"Afraid I have to do some work tonight, Mom." Jake extended his hand, waiting. "It was…interesting meeting you. And you are?"

Ignoring him, she merely pressed those lips together. The ones that tilted at the edges in a perpetual pout.

His mother said, "What is your name, darling? I'd love to see more of your work."

"Elena Eaton." She kissed his mother on the cheek and

thanked her before gliding away like a star.

"Isn't she lovely?" His mother watched her. "And she takes direction well. She could act." She raised an eyebrow at him.

"The answer is still no."

"It's a shame to let those good looks go to waste." His mother sniffed, but after a moment, she brightened. "Now where are those handsome policemen? I want to tell them everything I saw."

"Mom," Jake began in warning. "A serious crime was committed this evening. You will not waste officers' time flirting with them."

"The heck I won't," she replied with a petulant look. "My first husband was a police officer. I adore men on the force," she added with a wink.

"Look out number seven," Jake muttered, still watching Elena strut through the room. The black velvet dress she wore hugged her in all the right places. She was curvier than most of the fashionably thin women in the room. He liked what his mother called the full-figured 1950s look, though she wasn't plump, just nicely curved. But that was where the comparison stopped. Elena's blue eyes blazed with every word she spoke in that put-on Australian accent she was trying to pull off.

He should know. His mother could mimic a perfect Australian accent, thanks to intense voice coaching she'd had for one of her films. She'd received an Academy Award for best actress for that role about settling the Australian outback.

"This will be all over the press by tomorrow," his mother said, lowering her voice to him. "I'm so glad we were here when it happened. Such drama." She waved to two women. "Look, there's Aimee Winterhaus and Lele Rose, the designer who made me look gorgeous in *The Last Train from Paris*." She blew a kiss to the pair.

"That's not hard, Mom." Jake kissed her cheek. Being the son of Barbara Charles—who'd been born Batse Chonachowicz in Poland—had been like growing up with Auntie Mame.

He knew his mother worried about aging in an industry that valued youth. Acting—conveying a story, whether real or fictional—was what she had been born to do. She'd often told him the story of how her parents had come to the U.S. and she'd had her first commercial at the age of five, her first movie at six, and her first theatre role at seven. By the age of ten, she was a seasoned pro working with all the great actors and stealing scenes and hearts around the world. She simply loved acting and bringing stories to life.

He was her only child. Adopted, that is. Her third husband, Jakub Greyson II had insisted that they adopt the child her sister had borne out of wedlock. She'd died before Jake was even old enough to remember her, so Barbara Charles was the only mother he'd ever known.

His mother clucked her tongue. "I'm just sorry that poor girl had to suffer such a loss at the hands of thieves."

"Who?"

"Elena."

Jake tugged his earlobe, confused. What had Elena told her? "She wasn't robbed. Didn't you see the rocks on her ears?"

His mother gave him a stern look. "She designed the jewelry *parure* that Penelope Plessen was wearing."

"What are you talking about?"

"*Parure*. A suite of jewels. A set." She waved a graceful hand across her ears and red silk enrobed décolletage, as she called her ample cleavage. "Suitable for queens and empresses."

"I know what that is." His mother sometimes drove him crazy with the stories she constantly told. He shook his head. "She's a jewelry designer?"

"*Oy vey*, you're not listening."

"Her work—" He smacked his forehead. "Aw hell…Penelope Plessen. I didn't know."

"You should listen to your mother." She patted her blond hair and slid a conspiratorial gaze in his direction. "I think I need to consider another jewelry acquisition, wouldn't you say?"

"You have plenty, Mom."

She blew out an exasperated sigh. "How else am I going to get you two together? Did you see her figure? Grandchildren, for sure. Not like your skinny Jenny in Boston."

Jake stopped and stepped in front of his mother. "Mom. No. Not interested." A gorgeous woman like Elena was nothing but trouble. He should know.

She poked out her bottom lip in her famous pout. "Not even a little?"

"Not my type."

"As if the last one was."

"Jenny was a well-respected professor."

"And I admire that. I do. Your grandfather was a professor. It's just that she's not for you. And you should get over her."

"I have, Mom." Or had he? They'd dated for a couple of years before she'd moved to Boston to teach. She wasn't ready to commit, she'd told him, and he wasn't ready to follow her.

His specialty was investigation, and he'd made a name for himself as an investigator around the world. He told himself his hours weren't conducive to maintaining a relationship with Jenny or taking it to the next level.

Their relationship hadn't so much exploded as it had fizzled over the mountains and plains and oceans that separated them. Calls and texts became less frequent and more superficial, as if they both had something else on their mind, but called at the appointed hour because that's what they had agreed upon. Finally, Jenny called it quits, but the relationship had already withered and died.

A well-known producer angled his way toward them, catching his mother's eye. "Darling, we both have work to do," his mother said, patting his arm in a signal. "But tell the police to wait for me."

"I'm sure they will." Jake kissed her on the cheek before turning his attention back to the VIP room where the heist had occurred. Police officers had arrived, secured the building, and set about questioning guests, most of whom hadn't seen anything. He leaned against the VIP doorway, watching and listening.

His mother had lived in London when Jake was a teenager, and after completing public school, he'd decided to try something different. He'd become enamored with the Flying Squad, elite detectives who'd solved England's most high profile thefts, from the Great Train Robbery to Brinks-Mat, Millennium Dome, and Graff—all legendary heists. He'd apprenticed with the Flying Squad while he was studying law enforcement and a couple of years ago had worked to help catch the Over-the-Hill Gang in the Hatton Garden heist.

There'd been chatter in the network of villains and thieves centered on Los Angeles, but nothing had been pinned down. Old-fashioned sleuthing was often inadequate, while his work with digital investigating and surveillance was increasingly important.

Waiting for the police to question guests, Jake observed the celebrities and industry insiders. He'd look first to an inside job, to someone who knew the timing and lay-outs of the after-parties and of this one in particular. Fortunately, there would be ample photos and video of the evening to sift through.

He peered through the crowd, watching Penelope and Elena. Penelope might not have owned the jewelry she was wearing, but she was probably insured. As was standard procedure in the jewelry industry, she had undoubtedly signed documents rendering her liable if anything happened to the jewelry.

Most of the celebrities in attendance had either borrowed jewelry from major jewelers, or they were wearing their own. Bulgari, Tiffany, Cartier, and others had lent jewels to the stars in the room. But many stars owned their baubles. Elizabeth Taylor had been known for her collection, as was Ellen Barkin, who'd lately sold pieces from her collection. Today, it was Beyoncé, Kim Kardashian, and Mariah Carey who flaunted their expensive jewelry at parties like these.

Jake's gaze drifted to Elena again. Something didn't add up. Where had she acquired such costly stones? Who had insured her? And why had Elena lent such expensive pieces to Penelope?

He'd seen her talking to a server earlier. Who was the grungy guy? Jake pulled his phone from his pocket and zeroed in on him, snapping a quick photo. He swung around and caught an image of Elena, who was talking to Penelope, focusing on the nape of her neck beneath her short, sassy haircut. *Click.* She turned slightly. *Click.* Those expressive eyes. *Click.* He shoved his phone back into his pocket, feeling a little creepy for doing that.

Questions naturally ran through his mind. Either Penelope or Elena would undoubtedly make a claim, and he'd probably be called in to investigate this or other claims since he was on the scene. He lived to solve cases like this.

His adrenaline flowing, Jake scoured the restaurant, noting anyone who looked or acted suspiciously. Annoying him even more was the twinge in his chest he felt every time he looked at Elena.

4

AFTER GIVING HER statement to the police—*no, I didn't see anything*—Elena had stepped out of the VIP room at the rear of Bow-Tie to join Penelope, who was sitting on a sofa with their friends in the bar area. Verena, Scarlett, Fianna, and Dahlia were there commiserating with each other, while Lance and Johnny were seeing to guests.

Crumpled napkins littered the vintage wooden floor of the half-empty restaurant, and the atmosphere was thick with tension as people milled about with worried expressions. The glamour and excitement of the evening had been shattered. Once guests finished giving statements, they hurried out, anxious to leave the scene and move on to other parties. Except for those who had been robbed, who left just as quickly in a state of shock bound for home.

Feeling light-headed, Elena eased onto the edge of the couch next to Penelope, who pulled her close and hugged her. "We didn't expect the night to end like this, did we?" Elena said, leaning her head on Penelope's shoulder.

"I feel terrible," Penelope said. "If it had been only one guy, I bet I could've knocked that gun from his hand. But one of them had a barrel pressed against a woman's head."

"How horrible," Elena said.

Penelope rubbed her naked throat. "I shouldn't have allowed you to give me such an expensive set of jewelry to wear."

"Let you? I would've duct-taped it to you if you hadn't." Elena poked her in the side.

Fianna laughed, breaking the tension. "I could design something smashing with duct-tape."

"That's more Lele Rose," Penelope said, lifting a corner of her mouth. "Where is she, by the way?"

Dahlia spoke up. "I saw her leave with Barbara Charles. I overheard Aimee say they were going to the *Vanity Fair* party or the Governor's Ball. The night goes on for others."

Elena turned to Fianna and Penelope. "You two should go. This is an important night for you to make connections."

"Everyone I care about is right here," Penelope said, taking her hand and squeezing it. "We're in this together."

"I won't be celebrating until those villains are captured," Fianna said, tossing her hair over her shoulder. "How dare they hurt my friends and get away with it."

Stefan slid a hand over Penelope's shoulder, and she brushed her face against his skin. "I shouldn't have left your side, love," he said, rubbing Penelope's arm.

"You were only gone a few minutes. I'm afraid I ducked

into the VIP room and lost your other guard. I wasn't thinking, and it all happened so fast."

"That shouldn't have been your concern," Stefan said, caressing her shoulder. "You were here to have a good time and network."

Elena watched them, pleased that Stefan was here for her now. They'd been nearly inseparable since they'd reconnected at the dreadful incident during Fashion Week in New York. She sighed and pressed a hand against her rumbling stomach.

As for her, she'd go home alone and deal with it. She'd dated a few guys in Los Angeles, but she rose early to open her shop, and they'd wanted to party all night. Why couldn't she meet an adult with good manners? He didn't have to be jaw-dropping handsome—though she wouldn't turn that down, of course.

"Anyone hungry?" Lance approached them with a plate of hot empanadas. "Scarlett's mom whipped up some comfort food for us. Green chile pepper, corn, and saffron."

Scarlett's eyes widened as she plucked one with a napkin. "I'm starving." She slid another one toward Elena.

Isabel Sandoval emerged from the kitchen, wiping her hands on her white apron. She'd been working with Lance in the kitchen since Bow-Tie had opened, and her specialty, Spanish empanadas, had become a popular item on the menu.

Isabel smoothed an arm around her daughter. "So

relieved you weren't in the middle of that, *nena*."

"It was close, though," Scarlett said, hugging her mother. "Glad you're okay, too." She took a bite. "Mmm. Delicious, Mamá."

"Here, everyone, eat while they're hot." Isabel scooped up a couple of the delicacies she'd made and gave them to Penelope. "You've been through so much this past year. You're a brave woman."

Penelope laughed uneasily. "That's life in the fast lane, my mother says."

"We're slowing down a little to enjoy the scenery," Stefan said. "After she wraps her first season, we'd planned to get in some spring skiing at my cabin in Mammoth."

Elena loved watching Penelope and Stefan together. And Verena and Lance, and Scarlett and Johnny. Even Dahlia and Fianna had boyfriends now, though the guys traveled a great deal, so Elena still did a lot of things with her girlfriends.

She took a bite of Isabel's treat—they were good, and she realized she'd hardly eaten the entire day, except for a few miniature desserts and champagne. She'd lost her appetite, but she knew she should have something before she went home. She'd been working so hard she hadn't been to the market, and her fridge was absolutely empty.

Seeing Isabel reminded her that she should call her parents. They weren't on social media as much as Penelope's parents, but she'd have to call them as soon as she returned home. Her mother had grown up in San Diego and had met her dad there, who'd been visiting friends. *Love at first wave,* her dad always joked.

Their first date had been on surfboards, and he'd stayed as long as his visa would allow him to. When he'd asked her to marry him, she'd quickly accepted.

Her mother, Honey, was born in San Diego into a big, rambunctious family—the Bays—which was why she said she fell for her dad. Gabe reminded her of her own family. When Elena was little they'd moved back to care for his father in Sydney, Australia, where Gabe had grown up. Elena had picked up more of her mother's American accent, so people often wondered exactly where she was from. In fact, she wondered that herself.

Elena nibbled, finding it hard to relax after such a jarring evening. Once she went home, she'd be alone, and being on her own right now bothered her. Lance and Isabel returned to the kitchen to clean up, while Johnny catered to the few others guests who remained. Finally, she and her friends began to yawn.

"This is going to be all over the news tomorrow," Verena said. "We should all get some rest if we can."

Stefan and Penelope offered to take her home. She got into the black SUV with them, and they took her home to her cozy, ivy-covered vintage apartment a couple of blocks off Robertson Boulevard.

As they drove, they spoke little, each of them reflecting on the evening. Penelope was still shattered—being held up at gunpoint, and losing Elena's priceless set of jewelry—but Stefan was her rock. Elena had no one. After arriving at her eight-unit Spanish-style apartment building, Stefan walked Elena to her apartment to make sure she got in okay.

"Good-night," he said, making sure her doors were locked.

Penelope was lucky to have him, though Elena wasn't jealous. She just wondered if there was anyone out there for her.

She sank onto the amethyst-colored duvet covering her bed, still stunned. This night should have ended in a celebration, not like this. Elena's phone vibrated, and she glanced at the message. It was her cousin Coral again. *Saw the news on social media. Penelope's necklace was STOLEN???*

She tapped a message back. *Afraid so. Need to call my folks and break it to them. Please, don't tell them yet.*

After texting back and forth with Coral, she slipped out of her high heels and carefully removed her dress, and then got into bed and called her parents. They weren't angry, which made Elena cry even more. They were only concerned about her and relieved that she hadn't been injured—or worse.

As Elena explained the situation, her parents were quiet, taking in the loss. Finally, her mother spoke. "Want to come home for a visit, sweetie?"

"I have to stay and see this through." *Whatever that*

means, she thought. The payment on the funds she'd borrowed would be due soon, and without the sale of the jewelry Penelope had worn, or the uptick in sales she'd hoped for, she might be out of business soon.

This was a mess of her own making.

Tomorrow would be hell, too.

Burrowing under the covers, she tried to sleep, but she could only toss all night. Her mind wouldn't be quieted and every muscle in her body ached from the stress and shock.

The next morning, Elena pulled on a black knit dress and Tory Burch flats, made coffee, and filled her thermal cup to go. Just like any other morning, she set out to walk to her shop on Robertson Boulevard.

Only today was different.

Instead of enjoying the sunny morning and facing the day with enthusiasm as she usually did, she forced herself to put one foot in front of the other, feeling traumatized from her loss. While the full financial trauma hadn't yet hit her, the emotional loss of her labor of love was achingly palpable. Especially because those had been Sabeena's diamonds and in her family for generations. To her, they were priceless.

She walked to the rear door of her shop. Clicking her key in the lock and tapping the security system—double checking around her as she did—she stepped inside her little jewel box of a boutique.

Tiffany had robin's egg blue, Hermès had orange, and

Chanel had ebony black. She'd chosen rich royal blue, the color of sapphires. *The color of your eyes*, her father had always told her. Her parents weren't wealthy—her mother ran a small boutique near Bondi Beach, and her father had a surfing concession on the beach, but they'd regularly put away money and invested for their retirement. She'd originally borrowed money to open the shop, and had paid them back in less than two years. This time was different.

Against the Russian blue crystal chandeliers and thick azure carpet, pops of deep fuchsia added a touch of whimsy. So did fuchsia orchids and pillows, as well as a bold purplish-pink swoosh on her logo. A cobalt blue velvet love seat and chairs created an intimate salon atmosphere. A low glass cabinet doubled as a coffee table, and framed cabinets on the walls held her different collections. The result was modern and elegant—just liked her designs.

Her workbench was tucked into a closet-sized room with a wide glass window looking into the shop. She had a deep lapis blue velvet drapery pulled across it to hide it from view when clients came in and matching draperies across the front of the salon.

After withdrawing her pieces from the safe, she set up her displays. Sounds of street traffic filtered in, and she could hear rising chatter outside on the sidewalk, so she turned on her favorite jazz mix to drown out the noise and sooth her nerves. She lit a lavender candle that Fianna had given her, but doubted that aromatherapy would help much in this case.

Numbly going through the motions to keep her mind off the robbery, she arranged lacy necklaces similar to the one she'd designed for Penelope. They were less elaborate and had fewer gemstones, but still had plenty of sparkle and style. She loved the opulence of Indian jewelry, though she designed in several different styles. Orchestrating her business for post-Academy Awards exposure, she'd already photographed the Penelope-styled necklaces and uploaded images for sale on her website. Satisfied, she locked the case.

Her phone buzzed and she withdrew it from her purse. It was a text from Fianna next door.

Fianna: Are you at the shop?

Elena: Setting up.

Fianna: Look outside.

Elena stepped to the front of the shop and pushed open the drapes, revealing a mob of media blocking the sidewalk and pressed to the front of her shop. Anxiety seized her, and she felt light-headed. This was far beyond anything she had planned for. She mouthed the words, ten minutes, held up her hands, and let the drapes fall back.

Elena: OMG!

Fianna: They hit me early, but really want you.

Elena: Too many to fit inside!

Fianna: All they want to talk about is the robbery :(

Elena: Ta :(

Her heart pounding, she quickly collected herself. She'd prepared for publicity by hiring one of her cousins, Coral's sister Poppy, who was going to school at the nearby Annenberg School at the University of Southern California. Poppy had eagerly written press releases and disseminated images to major media outlets in anticipation of a successful night.

Elena had been prepared to give interviews about her jewelry, but discussing the robbery was outside of her comfort zone. She wasn't prepared to handle a disaster like this. More important, she was grieving the loss of her precious work and the financial devastation it would cause unless the case was solved and the jewelry returned. Buying insurance to protect jewelry off the premises was exorbitantly and prohibitively expensive. Penelope had promised to be responsible; Elena hoped she really had enough coverage.

Wrapping her arms around her, she weighed her options. She could leave the drapes drawn and hide, go home and pull the covers over her head, or face the melee outside. Stacks of media material—press releases, images, and USB drives—were already arranged on a side table. Now more than ever she needed sales. Anything would help her bleeding finances. She'd really been counting on a substantial sale.

This wasn't how she'd imagined the morning after the Academy Awards party would be.

Yet as difficult as it was, she had to do it. Her stomach was knotted with nerves, but she had to face reality and do what she could. After guzzling her coffee and drawing a deep breath, she pushed open the front drapes.

5

ELENA'S HAND FLEW to her mouth and she let out a cry of relief.

Clad in yoga wear, Scarlett stood at the front of Elena's shop, pressing her fingers against the glass while media people loudly complained behind her.

"Hey, we were here first," yelled a guy in a baseball cap and torn t-shirt. "Get in line."

"Back off," Scarlett said, throwing up her flat palm. "I'm her attorney."

"What's she got to hide?" asked another.

Shoving the accordion security gate aside, Elena hurriedly unlocked the door.

"I've never been so glad to see you," Elena said, pulling Scarlett inside and quickly locking the door behind her. She held up two fingers. Two minutes.

Or peace. *Whatever.*

"That's a rabid bunch out there," Scarlett said, brushing wisps of hair from her flushed face. "Completely *loco*. All on deadline and full of questions you probably can't answer. I was driving back from yoga when I saw the mob, so I stopped and ran over. Thought you could use some help."

"You have no idea," Elena said, hugging her. "Fianna texted and warned me. Said all they want to know about is the theft."

"Stick to the facts." Scarlett pulled the elastic band from her tawny blond hair to readjust her ponytail. "You don't really know anything and you can't guess."

"The only thing I can talk about is my jewelry." Elena motioned to the media material. "They can take those."

Scarlett twisted her mouth to one side. "That's not what they want. They want sensationalism, but you won't rise to the bait, understand? They're just doing their job, but anything you're uncomfortable answering, don't. I'll step in."

Elena nodded, thankful that Scarlett was here. "Are we ready?"

Scarlett scooped up the media material and opened the door. Charging out, she took control. "You won't all fit inside, so Elena Eaton will take questions out here. Anyone who wants an interview, form a line to the right or give me your card."

Elena stepped outside. "Hello." Before she could add anything, video cameras whirred and the questions rolled out.

"Did you see who stole the necklace?"

"Who do you think might have stolen it?"

"How much is it worth?"

"Is it insured?"

"Do you think it was an inside job?"

"Hold it right there." Scarlett flung up her hands. "If you have questions about the theft, direct those toward the police. I have press material for anyone who wants it. Now, Elena will answer *non-theft* related questions *only*."

Amid grumbling, one woman shot up her hand and squeezed forward.

"Did you design the jewelry with Penelope in mind?"

"I designed the cascading choker for her, but I designed an entire line. Photos are in the press maternal." Elena relaxed a little.

"What's the value?"

"About three to five million dollars." *Maybe more.* Elena put on a brave smile, despite the sinking feeling in her stomach. It hadn't cost her even half that because she already had many of the precious stones, but her time to make the suite had been an enormous investment. She was low on inventory and had to forgo other opportunities due to the time commitment. Because of that, she'd made less last year than the two years before, but this was an investment in the future of her business.

"Cartier lost a lot more than that."

"I'm sure they did. But that's a lot for me." Elena waved her hand behind her. "This is my only shop."

"So where'd you get the money?"

Scarlett frowned. "That's irrelevant. Next."

Family, friends, bank loans... Elena felt sick just thinking about it. She tried not to let her confidence falter.

A short man in front asked, "What was your inspiration?"

"The ocean. I grew up in Sydney, so I've always lived near the sea. Working with Fianna Fitzgerald, we envisioned a glittering mermaid princess."

"Like Wonder Woman of the Deep," a reporter quipped.

"Could be a new franchise," another one said.

Laughter trickled across the crowd.

"That's right," Elena said, feeding into the moment. "I've worked with Lele Rose on costume design, creating one-of-a-kind jewelry to go with her designs." She named a couple of films she'd contributed to, and the reporters made notes.

Scarlett winked at her, so Elena continued talking about how she'd come to create the collection.

"Who are you dating?"

"What?" Elena was nonplussed. *Why did that matter?*

"There are pictures of you with Hugo Gutierrez."

"Hugo's just a friend. He bought a piece for his mother."

"Any other celebrities who own your jewelry?"

Elena gave the names of a few of her clients who had already mentioned her name in the media. Smaller pieces were sometimes mentioned in articles about a star's favorite things. She'd been lucky to have a few lines of press. But she withheld the names of other more private celebrities. Being down the street from the famous Ivy restaurant and next door to Fianna, she had her share of celebrity clients, like many stores in Los Angeles. It was an industry town, after all. She'd even designed silver charms bracelets for one A-list actor's twelve-year-old daughter's birthday party.

A woman in the back waved her hand. "What will happen if your jewelry isn't recovered?"

Elena froze. *Total, complete, devastation,* she wanted to scream. Instead, she bit her lip.

Scarlett nodded slowly to her.

Collecting her thoughts, she began. "It will be a real blow, not only financially, but also because that jewelry is like a piece of my heart. I chose every stone, set each one, laboring long into the night for months. Penelope stood for fittings as I draped it on her to get it just right. There was so much love that went into its creation. I had hoped to see it worn with joy by someone special for many years to come. To me, jewelry is an expression of love, beauty, and creativity. I would hate to see that lost."

"Do you think the thieves will melt it down and sell the diamonds?"

Elena knew that was a possibility. "I hope not," she said, her voice catching. "I hope it finds its way home."

She took a few more questions while Scarlett disseminated media releases and USB drives that held images and other background material. Scarlett took some requests for interviews and promised that someone would get back to them by end of day.

Inside the shop, Elena collapsed on a love seat.

Scarlett twisted open two bottles of water from Elena's small refrigerator and handed her one. "You did well."

"With your support," Elena said, touching her bottle to Scarlett's.

Later, Elena was at her work bench polishing a prong she'd repaired on an emerald-cut diamond wedding ring for a client when the front door buzzed again. She looked up and saw a young woman dressed in stylish blue jeans waving through the front window.

"Come in, welcome," Elena said, smiling as she opened the door. The woman had honey brown hair in long sisterlocks drawn into a topknot, showcasing sparkling diamond studs on her earlobes. About half-carat each, Elena suspected, brilliant-cut and very bright against her caramel skin. Discreet, good quality. Classy.

"Looking for something special?"

"Actually, I'm looking for Elena Eaton. Is she in?"

"You've found her."

The young woman looked surprised. "The designer who created Penelope Plessen's jewelry?"

"The one and only. And you are?"

"I'm Ruby."

Elena grinned. "Great name."

"My mom worked at a jewelry store when I was born." She pulled a small moleskin notebook from her stylish leather backpack. "I'm a writer with *SheBlogsFashion*. I was wondering if you'd like to talk about last night." She looked around. "Where is everyone?"

"You missed the early rush."

Ruby shook her head. "Reporters are still jammed in front of Tiffany, Cartier, and Bulgari on Rodeo Drive. Everyone is talking about the robbery last night. The robbers sure made a haul from the celebrities that were in that room."

Elena perched on the arm of the sofa. "Big names sell. And they probably lost a lot more than I did."

Ruby gazed around the salon. "I love your shop. It's like being inside a jewelry box."

"Have a look."

"Wow." Ruby shifted her backpack. "These are gorgeous pieces. I saw photos of the necklace Penelope wore, and it was incredible. I'm so sorry for your loss."

"Thanks. That means a lot to me."

"My mom still tinkers with vintage jewelry. Your work really has a different point of view." She peered into the cases. "I love the lacy, opulent design you did for Penelope, but you have some bold pieces, too."

"That's my hammered silver collection with coral and turquoise. The casual look is popular in the summer here."

Ruby made a note and moved on to the fine jewelry section.

"A lot my work is custom. So how'd you find me?"

"Shane Wallace told me about you."

"You know Shane?" Just hearing his name made Elena's skin prickle.

"Not that well. We're just neighbors. He lives below me in my building. He called, said he had a tip for me, and showed me some photos he had of Penelope. I was already covering the story for my blog, like everyone else, so I thought I'd check you out and see if you'd like to share your story."

Shane must have been snapping photos while he was working. Not that Elena could blame him with all the celebrities there. She'd been hoping for positive media attention, so she didn't feel like talking about the incident. But Ruby seemed different. "I'll make a fresh pot of coffee and we can talk."

They'd been chatting for about half an hour and were so engrossed that when the security buzzer sounded at the front door, they both jumped.

Jake was standing outside.

Of all people. Elena rose from the love seat and opened the door with reluctance.

"Why aren't you answering your business phone?" He stepped inside.

"Well, hello to you, too. I haven't heard it ring." Maybe she'd forgotten to turn off the message forwarding in her groggy state earlier.

Jake's presence seemed to take up half the space in the

tiny salon. He even looked uncomfortable. "The police are questioning someone they believe is behind the robbery."

"Thank goodness," Elena said. If she didn't dislike him so much, she could've kissed him. "Well, thanks for stopping by." She'd call the police to find out more, but she couldn't wait to get rid of Jake. She opened the door for him to leave.

Jake cocked his head. "Aren't you going to ask who?"

Exasperated by him, Elena blew out a breath. "I'll talk to the detective later."

He shook his head. "You don't understand. All signs point to an inside job."

"Inside where?" Elena paused with her hand on the door. "Inside Bow-Tie."

Elena's hand flew to her mouth. *How was that possible?*

"The police are questioning Johnny Silva." Jake drew out his name for emphasis.

Elena stared at him, and then she burst out laughing. "That's the most ridiculous thing I've ever heard."

Jake stared at her, while Ruby noted Johnny's name.

Catching her breath, she said, "There's no way Johnny was involved. What, did they arrest the first Latin guy they saw?"

"Oh, boy," Ruby said, scribbling more.

Elena put a hand on her hip. "Ruby is a blogger."

"He's only being questioned at this time." Jake threw a pointed look at Ruby. "Can we talk in private somewhere?"

"Does it look like I have a conference room in here? Just

say what you came to say. I'm busy."

Shifting from one foot to another, Jake hesitated. "I really think—" He stopped and glanced at Ruby.

"What?"

"You might need an attorney, too," he blurted out.

Ruby's mouth formed a silent O while Elena threw up her hands. She couldn't believe this guy. "What are you insinuating?" She advanced on him, her finger pointed at his chest.

Elena turned to Ruby. "Johnny Silva is a great guy and one of the founders of Bow-Tie. No way is he involved. Plus, he dates one of my best friends. An attorney."

Ruby sighed and nodded. "I completely understand." She crossed off Johnny's name in her notebook.

"I sure appreciate that," Elena said, relieved.

"I think I have everything I need," Ruby said, glancing between Elena and Jake.

"Call me later if you need any clarifications, Ruby. Really nice to meet you. And you should visit Fianna Fitzgerald to learn more about Penelope Plessen's dress. She's right next door. Tell her I sent you."

Ruby thanked her and left.

Elena whirled to face Jake. "You're unbelievable. Is that all you came for?"

He shifted on his feet and shrugged. "Look, I'm sorry about that. I wanted to see how you were doing, too."

"How'd you find me?"

"Looked you up online." He glanced around. "Nice place. So, is this it?"

He seemed to be attempting pleasantries. "I call it the international world headquarters."

"And this is all your work?"

"That's right." She watched as he peered into the glass cases holding her designs. Out of a tuxedo, he looked even more buff. He'd definitely spent hours working out or something to get in the shape he was in. The sleeves of his crisp white dress shirt were folded back, revealing muscular forearms, and his gray slacks rode his trim hips just right. His dark hair was cut short and he'd shaved the dark stubble that had lined his angular jawline the other night. Not bad, if you liked that sort of look. Averting her eyes, she tidied the remaining press material.

"How long have you been in business?" he asked.

"This is my fifth year here."

"Hmm. How'd you get started?"

"I've been designing since I was a kid. Reworking vintage costume jewelry at first. Selling simple pieces to friends. Then I studied at the G.I.A. in San Diego."

"You started young. What are you, about…?"

"More experienced than I look." She folded her arms. "Did you come here to ask my age?"

Jake rubbed his forehead. "Guess I deserved that."

"Surely your mother taught you better."

He grinned. "My mother? Indeed she did." He thumped

his fingers on the back of the velvet love seat.

Elena noticed a small cleft in his cheek. He had probably been a cute dimpled kid. She pushed the thought from her mind.

"Saw a throng of reporters in front of your place this morning."

"They were here when I arrived. Fortunately, Scarlett saw them, too. At least she stopped to help me handle them."

"Do you like to talk to the media?"

His questions were starting to annoy her. "It's part of building a brand."

Jake trailed a finger along a glass case. "I enjoyed meeting you last night. I know I can be kind of gruff in tense situations."

Her dad could be like that, too. "Is that an apology?" He seemed to be talking around something.

"Yeah, I guess it is. Please, let's start over." He held his hand out, his eyes trained on her. "Jake Greyson, pleased to meet you."

"Elena Larisa Eaton. Charmed." She shook his hand. His clasp was warm and solid, but not too strong. Not the aggressive bone-crushing, turning-their-hand-on-top move that some guys did. Or worse, the limp fish handshake. No, his was firm and honest. *You can tell a lot by a man's handshake*, her father had told her. Or in other cultures, by their bow. Still, some men had mastered the perfect handshake as part of the perfect deception. Yet she knew

Stefan was a friend of Jake's and seemed to hold him in high regard.

"Come here often?" Jake grinned again.

"Uh, yeah." She smiled, relaxing a little. He was a little corny, though. She watched as he shoved his hands into his pockets and shifted from one foot to another.

"Look, I—I wondered if…"

"Yes?"

"If you'd like to have dinner tonight?"

Elena took a half step back. That was absolutely the last thing she thought she'd hear come out of his mouth. "Um, sure." Inwardly, she winced. That was also the last response she thought she'd have. *God, I need help. Or at least, more coffee.*

"Okay then. Pick you up at your place at seven?"

"Um, sure."

Jake held out his phone. "Want to put your number in?"

She took it and tapped in her number and address before handing it back to him. *What am I doing?*

"Good, thanks," he said. "Well then, see you later." He ducked out of the salon, waving through the glass at her as he walked by.

Her phone rang and she saw it was Fianna. Answering it, she said, "Guess who just left my shop? And who I agreed to have dinner with tonight?"

"Hugo Gutierrez?" Fianna let out a little squeal.

"We're just friends." Elena twirled a short strand of hair

while she spoke. "Jake Greyson."

"Jake from last night?" Silence. "He *is* hot, but I didn't think you liked him."

"Neither did I." Should she cancel? Yet something about him intrigued her.

"Maybe you should close up early to get ready."

She suppressed a yawn. *If only...* "I'm still hoping for more customers today. I've already sold two necklaces that were smaller versions of Penelope's."

"I've had a good day, too. People are curious after reading the press. And thanks for sending Ruby over. She's taking some photographs now." Fianna paused. "Please tell me you're not wearing black."

"Maybe. I'm in mourning." She shifted the phone. "I'm going to look up Jake Greyson online."

"Always a good idea."

They hung up and Elena tapped Jake's name into the computer. A number of articles popped up. *Private Investigator to Kings and Presidents*, one read.

She sat back, dumbfounded.

Who *was* this guy?

6

JAKE GOT INTO his car and slapped his forehead. *Dinner with Elena Eaton?* "What the hell was I thinking?" he muttered to himself and started his car.

He'd built a successful career by not allowing his emotions to interfere with investigations. Although technically, he wasn't on an investigation. If the thieves were caught and the jewelry recovered—case closed. *If* they caught all parties involved.

Which was the reason for his visit to Elena's salon. He couldn't help his inquisitive mind. In his experience, people took crazy risks for glittery stones and the allure of instant wealth. Schemes to defraud insurance companies were also common, and it was his job to unmask the villains and recover the goods.

Sometimes the villains turned out to be beautiful women, too. Could Elena Eaton be one of them? He'd searched her vital statistics in his database, though not much had shown up. Yet, he'd seen her talking to a server at the party last night, Shane Wallace.

After calling Lance Martel, who was cleaning up at Bow-Tie, Jake had learned Shane's name and where he was from. Punching in this information, he'd discovered the guy was an Australian with a penchant for older woman with money and sparkly jewelry. Furthermore, he and Elena appeared to have been in San Diego about the same time several years ago. *Were they more than friends?*

Jake turned the ignition in his car and started for Penelope's home in the Hollywood Hills. Stefan had called and asked to meet him there. He had nothing but respect for Stefan, and had sent him a couple of his buddies from the club where he worked out to train as bodyguards. He'd once asked Stefan if he ever planned to practice law again, but he'd just laughed and told him the criminals could do without his services.

Which brought him back to Elena. Was she a victim of robbery, like Penelope, or was she involved in a scheme to defraud the insurance company? With looks like hers, she could talk men into anything, he'd bet. She'd looked amazing last night in that black velvet Jessica Rabbit dress that hugged her like a glove. Today, that knit thing she was wearing skimmed her curves just right. With those brilliant blue eyes, he'd fallen under her spell, despite his efforts.

All he'd gone to do was to look at her shop and ask her a few questions. Then he'd ended up asking her out to dinner.

He blamed his mother for putting that thought into his head last night. Barbara Charles was a firm believer in romance, and she thought he was sorely missing out on one of life's best pleasures.

Damn it. He'd just have to make the best of this dinner with Elena. He'd make it all business, that's what it would be. He'd get to the bottom of this relationship with Shane Wallace.

He'd also like to find out where she acquired her stones. Were they really of any value? He parked his Jaguar and got out.

"Jake, my man." Stefan invited him into Penelope's Spanish-styled home perched high in the Hollywood Hills. "Heck of a night, but glad you were there."

Jake gave him a hearty bro hug and looked around. "Great view," he said, looking straight through the wide glass expanse in the living room and out over the Los Angeles basin in the distance.

"Penelope's outside. This way."

Jake followed him, admiring the comfortable home. Land had become so expensive in Los Angeles that many homes of this vintage had been torn down, and McMansions—as imposing, block-style homes were often derisively called in L.A.—had been built in their place on lots too small for them.

They stepped onto the deck that wrapped around the hillside house.

"Perfect timing. Just finished my swim," Penelope said, emerging from the pool and flipping her blond and turquoise hair back.

"Nice meeting you again," Jake said, trying his best to keep his gaze at eye level. She was attractive, but he was respectful.

"Likewise. Under a little better circumstances today," she said as she toweled off and wrapped a Hawaiian print sarong around her yellow one-piece swimsuit. "Though not much," she added, shaking her head.

She was even more beautiful in person than in her photos, he thought, so he was pleased for Stefan, who really seemed to care for her. He watched the glances and small touches they exchanged, and the ease with which they communicated as he asked how her swim was, and she asked him how a phone call had gone. It looked a lot like love to him, though he was hardly a good judge of that.

Jake sat with them at a table near the pool.

Stefan asked, "Any leads?"

"It's early yet, though I've set the wheels in motion," Jake replied. One of the major insurance companies had already contacted him about engaging his company to investigate its loss.

"Stefan tells me you just returned from London," Penelope said, stretching her legs out.

"I closed out a case for a client." Jake rolled his sleeves back another fold. The sunny spring day was welcome after the dreary weather he'd had last week in London. "This was your first year to attend the Academy Awards, right?"

"You've done your homework," Penelope replied. "And you?"

"I often escort my mother, Barbara Charles. Between husbands," he added with a grin. "She's a member of the Academy and loves to see old friends." She'd won a Best Actress Award for a western when she was younger and a Best Supporting Actress Award more recently.

Penelope smiled. "I've always loved her work. I grew up watching her movies."

"So did I," Jake said. That line always brought a laugh and today was no exception. He liked his clients to feel at ease. Though Penelope wasn't a client. It would be her choice as to whether she wanted to open a claim. He had a contact at her insurance company and knew that if she did, they would engage him to investigate the claim. Stefan had asked him to come and explain the details.

Penelope rested her chin in her hand. "So you perform investigative services. How'd you get into that?"

"My father founded Greyson Insurance more than fifty years ago. That's what fueled my interest in insurance fraud investigations. Greyson Investigations is the company I started, so I work for a lot of different companies on high profile cases. Like this one."

"Jake likes to catch the bad guys," Stefan said, resting his arm across Penelope's shoulder.

"I read that you've been called the Sherlock Holmes of insurance fraud," she said.

Jake grinned. "That came from a zealous writer, I'm afraid."

"Don't be humble." Stefan brushed a wisp of turquoise hair from Penelope's lashes. "He's *that* good. Heads of state use his services."

"What's your secret?" she asked. "I hope it's not the seven-percent solution."

"Definitely not. I'm thorough, I have an experienced team, and we have a lot of contacts," he said. *On both sides of the law.* Thieves liked to brag, and that trait often tripped them up.

Jake rubbed the back of his finger across his jaw, looking between Stefan and Penelope, and trying to gauge her desire to proceed with a claim. "Are there any questions you have at this point?"

Penelope spoke up. "I have a jewelry rider on my insurance policy, mainly for my grandmother's jewelry that I inherited. Does that mean this is covered?"

"Depends. You probably have a limit." Jake said. "Major jewelers like Harry Winston or Tiffany carry block coverage that has broad coverage terms. After visiting Elena in her shop, I would guess that she doesn't carry that." He hesitated, knowing he was treading into sensitive areas. "Did she ask you for proof of valuable articles coverage, or did you check your policy?"

"No."

"I'll check your policy if you'd like," Jake said, trying to soften the blow he was fairly certain was coming. "Did you sign an agreement to assume financial responsibility for damage or theft?"

"I sent her an email and told her I'd be responsible if anything happened. I knew I had insurance. But I didn't know how much the pieces were really worth. I heard on the news it has a value of at least three million. Maybe five."

"Did she tell you that?"

Penelope looked crestfallen. "I didn't ask."

"Then that has yet to be established." What he didn't say—because Penelope and Elena were friends—was that he had his doubts about the diamonds. What was someone with a little shop on Robertson that was barely large enough to swing a bat in doing with a multi-million dollar set of jewelry? Nothing he saw in the shop would support a trade like that. In his experience, so-called friends screwed over people more often than he liked to share.

Penelope shifted. "I really feel like Elena should be here. We can work this out together, I'm sure. She's one of my best friends."

"You need to know where you stand." Jake exchanged a sad look with Stefan. They'd both seen friendships ruined over things like this. "First, we'll have to investigate to see if there was an appraisal, and if so, was a valid one. There's a lot of room for fraud, I'm afraid."

"Elena's not like that," Penelope said sharply.

"I'm not saying she is. But appraisers have been known to overstate value or swap stones."

She looked alarmed. "What's the chance of that happening?"

Jake narrowed his eyes in thought. "If the appraiser is suspect, she'll have to produce receipts for the stones and prove they were used in the jewelry that was stolen. Otherwise, your claim can't be paid and you'll be personally liable for whatever value is agreed upon. Or you go to court."

"Of course I'm liable," Penelope said quietly. "I borrowed the jewelry, so it's my responsibility." She raised her famous tawny eyes to him, and he could see the worry in them. "You'll check on the coverage?"

"I will." Jake felt sorry for her. He didn't know what she was worth, but Stefan had said she'd lost a lot of runway work the past year after nearly being shot at Fashion Week in New York. She had a television show in development, but it hadn't launched yet.

Stefan clasped Penelope's hand. "What should she do in the future if a stylist suggests she borrow jewelry?"

"Only work with major jewelers, or borrow pieces that are within the limits of your coverage. Sometimes insurance companies increase limits for an event, or celebrities buy short-term coverage through Lloyd's of London or another syndicate."

"Sounds expensive," Stefan said.

"It can be," Jake agreed.

"And the alternative?" Penelope asked.

"Don't wear expensive jewelry," Jake said.

"While I agree in principle," Penelope said, leaning forward earnestly, "that's not how the fashion business works. Or the entertainment industry. The media is looking for the most amazing, over-the-top fashion and jewelry to photograph and put on covers. That builds careers on both sides. For the model or actress, as well as for the fashion and jewelry designers. Elena, Fianna, and I were all helping each other. Furthering each other's career."

Jake sighed. "As long as you're covered—and there's no fraud—then you're okay. The insurance company carries the burden. If not, you're liable. You'll have to work that out with Elena."

"Let's hope the police catch the bastards," Stefan said. "Then everyone will be happy."

Jake smiled, though he had his doubts. It was a quick, well-executed job by a group who knew what they were doing. They'd fence the pieces, or pop the stones. The best ones knew not to make any fast moves to escape detection. Still, he'd already put out inquires. If they could get a lead, or security film from a nearby business, they could make some headway.

The three of them talked a little more, and Penelope thanked him for his advice before he left. As he wound down the hill, he turned over the events of the evening in his mind.

Several disturbing points nagged him. The presence of Shane Wallace, a small-time criminal with shady ties, and the new after-party venue of Bow-Tie. Then there was Johnny Silva, the restaurant partner that everyone seemed to know.

He'd met Johnny briefly before—the night of the robbery and when he'd taken cooking classes with Stefan from Johnny's partner, chef Lance. Jake had discovered that Johnny had grown up in a barrio of Los Angeles and could have questionable connections. However, Jake had ferreted out his share of white collar criminals from Ivy League universities, too.

Crossing Hollywood Boulevard, his thoughts turned to Elena, whose activities raised the most questions. She was also the one he hadn't been able to get out of his mind for reasons other than purely professional interest. Yet, he was a pro, and he would conduct himself like one.

Turning onto Sunset Boulevard toward his home in Santa Monica, he told himself he could handle Elena. He'd get exactly what he needed from her at dinner. That had been a good idea after all, he thought, congratulating himself on asking her out.

7

AFTER JAKE LEFT, Elena had one of the busiest sales days she'd had in months, which she was thankful for because it kept her mind off the robbery and brought in some much needed cashflow.

By noon, Elena had spoken to an assistant of Aimee Winterhaus and given her details of the jewelry suite. *Fashion News Daily* was still running the cover of Penelope and wanted to confirm information before publication.

Just as Elena hung up, a call from an editor at *Town & Country* magazine in New York came in, asking her to send one of her Penelope necklaces for a photography shoot they were planning for the big fall edition. Elena was thrilled and agreed, and then immediately put in a call to Scarlett to ask about how she should go about lending pieces now.

The thought of suffering any more losses was more than she could imagine, and certainly more than she could handle—financially or emotionally.

In the midst of it all, Fianna dropped off a double green

smoothie from Whole Foods for her, and she was sipping it in between customers when the phone rang and Penelope's photo appeared on her screen.

"Hi Penelope," she said. "Have you recovered?"

"Somewhat. I slept in and had a swim." Penelope paused.

Elena detected an anxious note in her voice. "What's wrong?"

"What happened last night…I'm just shattered over it. Stefan called Jake and he came by—"

"Jake was here, too. We're going to dinner tonight."

"Oh," Penelope said, sounding a little surprised. "Anyway, he's checking my coverage, but in case the police don't recover it, I want you to know that I consider myself responsible."

Elena bit her lip. Even though she'd had a good day, the robbery loomed over her like a storm cloud. "The police *have* to catch them." She squeezed her eyes shut. Every time she thought of what she'd lost, she grew sick inside.

"But if they don't—"

"No, they *will*." Her voice caught, and she took a sip of the smoothie just as another customer buzzed the front door for entry. "Penelope, I can't talk about this right now. But thank you for offering."

"We'll work it out. I know we can." Penelope's words tumbled out. "You were there for me when I needed you in New York and Copenhagen during that whole mess. I don't want to lose our friendship over this."

Elena smiled sadly into the phone, remembering. "Neither do I."

"I'll think of something, I promise." Worry edged Penelope's voice.

"Let's just hope they find the jewelry."

Ending the call, Elena buzzed in a customer and put on a pleasant face for them. Yet inside, she felt destroyed, suspended in agony as if this were a nightmare she'd wake from. But it was all too real.

Earlier, she'd called her insurance company and discovered she was woefully underinsured. Next time—if she could somehow remain in business if the police didn't find the thieves—she'd make sure both she and the borrowing party were covered.

But who would have ever imagined that with security all around at an Academy Awards after-party, her precious jewelry would vanish like smoke?

Later that day after closing her shop, Elena walked to her apartment to get ready for dinner with Jake. Walking was her therapy time, when she shed the troubles of the day. But today's troubles were not so easily shed.

As she strolled past trimmed yards with jasmine clinging to the fences and low walls, she inhaled the sweet scents of spring. Roses were blooming, too, vying for attention in vibrant shades of pink, yellow, and lavender. She stopped to smell the most voluptuous red rose that arched toward her, drawing a moment of pleasure from the scent. Inspiration for her designs came from many places, but often from nature. Continuing her walk, she nodded to mothers with children and old couples holding hands who passed her on the sidewalk.

What a day, she thought, trying to focus on the positive. By closing, she'd sold six pieces from the new collection, and set up three private consultations with new clients. She'd received orders from her website, too.

Besides that, emails from writers working on stories about the robbery had poured in. She'd quickly called Poppy for help, and turned over that publicity task to her. Scarlett had supplied statements about the incident approved for publication. *No more mistakes*, Elena thought, chastising herself.

She hadn't heard a word from the police and that disturbed her. If not for her date with Jake tonight, she'd probably go home and hide under the blankets in bed again. It was funny, she hadn't particularly liked Jake at first, but he was growing on her. Touching the palm of her hand, she recalled the solid feel of his handshake. Even his anxiety in asking her out was endearing. Her male friends had told her that her directness made men feel uncomfortable. Was that why Jake seemed nervous?

Elena smiled to herself. She certainly liked his mother, Barbara Charles.

Once inside her apartment, she'd just put her bag down

and slipped off her shoes when a tap sounded on the door.

"Hi, Poppy." Her younger cousin's silky blond hair was slipping from a messy bun, and she was dressed in yoga gear.

"I got here as soon as I could after my last class," Poppy said, her arms laden with small gift boxes and bags. "I just picked up these at the printers. They turned out really nice."

"These are beautiful, thanks." Elena inspected the marketing materials she'd asked Poppy to oversee. The thick, opalescent sapphire-colored gift bags and boxes were inscribed with Elena's silver logo and fuchsia swoosh. She ran her hand over the silky paper. "I love how rich it feels."

"I'm sending out press releases to bloggers tomorrow," Poppy said, excitement in her eyes. "I also created a list of FAQs—frequently asked questions—for your approval." She handed it to Elena. "Let me know if it's okay."

"Did you learn this at school?" Elena glanced at it.

Poppy nodded. "I'm thinking about opening a PR company after school. Or maybe I'll try to work for one and get some experience first."

"Lots of opportunities here."

"Have to run," Poppy said. "I'll send out social media messages tomorrow. Let me know what else you need. This is fun!" After a quick hug, she trotted out the door.

Elena was so pleased with Poppy's help. By giving her some of the time-consuming marketing and clerical work, she'd increased her more valuable design time. And she loved Poppy's enthusiasm.

After checking the time, Elena went to change. She stood in front of her closet deciding what to wear. Fianna's words about wearing black rang in her mind.

Jake had been wearing dress slacks, a white dress shirt, and polished dress shoes, so she decided to dress up a little, even though it was Monday night. She wondered where they might go. Maybe to Mr. Chow or Spago, some of her favorite restaurants beside Bow-Tie. Or a chic café in West Hollywood.

Smiling with anticipation, she reached for a slim dress the color of tanzanite, a purplish-blue that was one of her favorite colors and deepened the blue in her eyes. She added a pair of tanzanite earrings and tucked her short hair behind her ears to showcase them.

For good luck, she clasped on a bracelet from her new collection—the one everyone was now calling the Penelope collection—and stepped into high heels.

The doorbell rang and she pressed a hand against her heart, forcing herself to saunter to the door and not race to answer it like the kid she felt like inside.

As she opened the door, her smile faltered. Jake had changed. He wore dark jeans and a casual knit shirt. He still looked good—too good in those jeans and the shirt stretched across his muscular chest, in fact—but now she felt completely overdressed.

"Oh, wow," he said, hooking a thumb into his jeans. "You look *really* nice."

His gaze wrapped around her and he obviously liked what he saw.

"And you...changed," she said, waving her hand.

Jake shrugged. "I met my trainer after work and didn't feel like dressing up again."

"That's okay." She studied her keys, thinking. That *should* be okay, right? Had she only known. Not that he needed to call her to coordinate wardrobes. Now she was feeling conflicted. *Stop it.* She'd just suffered an enormous loss. What did a trivial thing like this matter? *Not at all.*

He took a step toward her and touched her am. "You still with me?"

"It's been a long twenty-four hours and I'm starving." She shut the door to her apartment and locked it.

"I had a late lunch. How about Starbucks? They have sandwiches and we can walk over." He clicked his car key fob. The lights and locks on a sleek, charcoal gray Jaguar sedan parked at the curb responded.

Elena gazed longingly at the car. She hadn't planned on hiking in five-inch heels.

"It's not far, come on."

"You can't be serious." She hadn't even left her front step and already this date was going downhill fast. Holding up a finger, she said, "I'll change shoes."

As Jake's gaze traveled down her legs to her shoes, he raised his eyebrows. "Those are incredible shoes. Can't walk in them?"

"Not as far as you have in mind." Yoga pants and flip-flops were starting to sound awfully good. "The nearest Starbucks is eight to ten blocks from here."

"Are you sure?"

"I live here." Elena let out a long sigh. *Was he really this clueless?* "Chances are they'll be sold out of sandwiches at this time of night. But I have to eat something. Come in and I'll make pasta. You can watch if you're not hungry. Or leave if you want." She turned back to the door and inserted her key. *Insufferable man.*

Jake bounded back up the steps and caught the doorknob in his hand. "Wait. I know of someplace we can go."

"I'm not walking to Denny's diner either." She turned the key. Tonight, all she wanted was some semblance of kindness. Her emotions were too raw to have to deal with an oaf.

He held firm to the knob. "Don't change. You look so…" He waved his hand over her outfit. "We'll take the car."

Elena glanced over her shoulder. "I'm not eating a day-old sandwich."

"I can do better than that, trust me." Jake offered her his hand. "I've been told I'm abrupt. Sometimes I'm short on social graces."

"Did your mother tell you that? Or was it your last girlfriend?"

"Ouch," he said, wincing. "Both actually. My mind is

often somewhere else. But I'm working on it." He clicked open the car.

Elena took a tentative step from the door and placed her hand in his outstretched palm. His grip felt strong and sure, but it would take more than this to regain her confidence in him.

As he helped her into the car, she couldn't help but think this was already one of the stranger dates she'd been on.

Ten minutes later, Elena found herself in the open air rooftop restaurant of the Waldorf Astoria, looking out over the lights of Beverly Hills and Century City. Jazz music and the subtle scent of expensive perfume wafted through the air. The dress was upscale casual, so they both fit in. Not that Elena cared anymore. She was over that.

The hostess seated them on an outdoor sofa in front of a wide fireplace flanked by vertical wall gardens of tropical greenery. The night was cool, but sitting by a crackling fire and surrounded by towering gas heaters, Elena felt comfortable in her sleeveless dress.

Voices murmured around them, and laughter tinkled against raised glasses in the simple celebration of life. The good life. A waitress greeted them, and Jake ordered two glasses of cabernet sauvignon. Feeling famished, she ran a finger down the menu.

Elena looked up. "I'll have the tuna tartare with avocado and ginger, the lobster burger with gruyere and green chili dressing, and sweet potato fries. And change my wine to a

Vouvray."

A smile played on Jake's full lips. "You were hungry. And you have good taste. I like a woman who eats."

"We can share if you're tempted." She caught his dark gaze in the flickering firelight and saw an emotion sweep across his face, but she couldn't say what is was. Jake Greyson was an enigma.

After the wine was served—red for him, white for her—he touched his glass to hers. "Here's to recovering your jewels," he said in a serious tone.

His wine reflected the firelight like garnets. "Amen to that," she said, studying him over the top of her glass as she took a sip of the chilled wine. "I enjoyed meeting your mother last night."

"The two of you seemed thick as…well, you know."

Elena smiled, though she ached inside at her loss. "You must have had fun growing up with her."

"She's special, that's for sure. And infuriatingly majestic at times." A fond smile lit his face. "But wise and attentive when it counts. We're pretty thick, too."

Elena could tell he had a special relationship with his mother. That was a good sign, she thought. Although Barbara looked youthful for her age, she assumed that she must have had Jake fairly late in life. Judging from subtle laugh lines, she guessed Jake to be about thirty-five.

The food was delivered to the low table in front of them and Elena ate ravenously, not having eaten much since the night before. She'd nibbled on a scoop of caviar, a tiny dessert, and an empanada yesterday, and had a smoothie for lunch, but it hadn't been nearly enough. "Help me with the fries, at least."

Jake did, and then he sampled her tuna tartare and lobster burger at her insistence. He eased back against the sofa, watching her. She felt his eyes on her, and when she crossed her legs and brushed his thigh, he didn't move. Neither did she, enjoying the closeness of this interesting man.

Smart, dangerously handsome, with a heart that loved his mother—no wonder women overlooked his lapse of manners. Idly, she wondered if he were trainable... Not that she cared to, she told herself. She'd never been into rehabilitation. But he *was* nice to look at.

As she sipped her wine, Jake leaned forward, the firelight dancing in his dark mocha eyes and his black hair glistening in the flickering light.

He held his glass aloft, pondering the color thoughtfully. Slowly, he said, "I really hope the police recover your jewelry."

"Aren't you paid to investigate claims?"

He touched her hand. "This is one case I'd rather not investigate."

Elena glanced down and responded with a flick of her finger against his. Just then, a portly man bumped against Jake's arm, splashing wine onto his dark jeans.

"Oh, no." Elena grabbed her dinner napkin and began to dab wine from the fabric, noting his muscular thigh as she did. Probably a runner, she thought, lingering on his leg.

Jake leaned forward, grinning. "That's good, thanks."

Elena inclined her head as she pressed the napkin. "Why wouldn't you want to investigate?"

"Isn't it obvious?" He took the napkin from her and placed his hand over hers. "You don't have to do that. Although it was nice."

A thrill raced through her at his touch, and her face grew warm. Feeling conflicted, she wasn't entirely sure that she wanted the conversation to go in this direction now. "Is there anything you can do to help the police?"

"There's a lot you can do."

Neither of them moved their hand.

A smile tugged at his lips. "That's an amazing collection you created. If the stones were certified, they'd be numbered."

"Well, they're not." Elena bit the edge of her bottom lip with her teeth. Gemstones had a history, and these were no exception.

Jake frowned slightly. "Where did you find such high quality stones?"

Elena shrugged. "Here and there. I always look for unique gemstones." To her, each stone had a personality and a story—especially these. "Some have histories, having adorned the fingers and encircled the necks of beautiful women throughout the ages."

Picking at the last of her food, she grew silent. Other gemstones and jewelry had been smuggled out of countries sewn into children's stuffed animals and ladies' hemlines, and they were used to pay for safe passage for their anguished owners who clung to the hope of better lives.

Jake seemed to carefully process every word she said. "Did you have the set appraised?" he asked.

She shifted with discomfort. "I didn't exactly have time. I was working on it up to the last minute."

He raised an eyebrow. "You let jewelry of that caliber walk out of your shop without a valuation?"

"I have a good idea of the value." Elena pressed her lips together. Unfortunately, he had a strong point, and it wasn't lost on her. "How long do you think it might take for the police to track down the thieves?"

"Assuming they can, you mean. The police are investigating now." He looked from one side to another. "I have a retired police force captain who joined the company, so we're getting a lot of insights on guests and people who worked the party." Jake's eyes lingered on her as he spoke.

"Insights?" The way he was looking at her with his dark gaze made her neck tingle. "I thought you weren't investigating the case."

"I said I didn't want to." He squeezed her hand and gave a deep sigh. "People aren't always what they appear to be. Are they, Elena?" He quirked up a side of his mouth.

Sliding her hand from his, Elena sat back. "Excuse me, but that sounded like you were accusing me of something."

He chuckled. "It's cute, but you can cut the fake accent with me." Jake grinned. "I know what a real Australian accent sounds like. My mom took voice lessons and she nailed it in a part she played."

Her lips parted, but she was at a momentary loss for words. "Do you have any shred of decency or manners?"

"Come on, Elena. I know you were born in San Diego and attended the G.I.A. What I don't know is how you made the leap into such high-priced trade so quickly."

She folded her arms. "Obviously you haven't read the rest of your reports," she said. "I grew up in Bondi Beach in Sydney. If you'd stuck to Googling me like most normal people do, you'd know that." She ignored the rest of his absurd comment that sounded suspiciously like he was questioning her ethics.

It was his turn to be surprised. "Oh, that might explain it…" His face flushed. "You Googled me?"

"Of course, I always look up a guy before I go on a date with him."

Jake's eyes widened. "Who said this was a *date*?"

"You asked me out to dinner," she said, slowly articulating every word.

Jake ran a hand over his hair. "I can see how you might have interpreted it that way. But I just need to get more details about the case."

Embarrassed and angry, Elena snatched her purse and pulled out her wallet. "Then I guess this *meeting* is over. How much do I owe you for dinner?"

Jake pushed her wallet back into her purse. "No, I've got this. But I didn't mean that I wouldn't *want* to go out on a date with you sometime."

"Is that supposed to make me feel better?" She stood. "I'll find my own way home. And do me a favor," she added. "Delete my number."

As she stalked through the restaurant, she heard him call her name, but she couldn't stop. The events of the last twenty-four hours crashed over her, making her feel vulnerable. She pushed the elevator button, praying it would arrive before he did.

She stepped inside the elevator, and as the doors closed she saw Jake racing to catch her.

Never again, she promised herself, would she get involved with a man who made her feel less the person she knew she was. When the elevator doors slid open, she marched to the front of the hotel and got into a waiting taxi.

Never again, she repeated under her breath, as frustration and fatigue finally overwhelmed her.

8

EXHAUSTED AFTER HER non-date with Jake, Elena barely had time to kick off her shoes and slip off her dress before she fell into bed. It was only nine o'clock, but she'd hardly slept the night before. However, she hadn't been asleep long when her phone buzzed on the pillow next to her. She ignored it.

It buzzed again.

"Better not be Jake," she muttered, fumbling in the dark. Squinting against the screen's light, she saw a message pop up.

Mum: Are you awake, sweetie?

Elena: I am now.

Mum: Ok, I'm calling you…

A few seconds later, the phone rang. "What's up, Mum?"

A silence ensued, and Elena thought she could hear her mother sniffing as though she were crying. "Mum? Are you there?" She bolted upright in bed. *What's wrong?*

Honey Eaton was the stable rock of the family, and Elena could count the number of times she'd seen her mother cry on one hand. "*Mum!*" She could hear a commotion in the background.

"Oh sweetie, your dad is resting, but he went into cardiac arrest at the beach. He'd been surfing and he collapsed. Fortunately, he was out of the water."

"A heart attack..." Elena was at a loss for words. A hundred questions roared through her mind.

"He's going into surgery."

"Is it...serious?" Elena could hardly draw the breath to form the words.

"Yes." A long hesitation ensued. "He's really weak. We'll know more soon."

She ran a hand over her face. All her troubles suddenly seemed minuscule in importance. *Jewelry, publicity, sales, robbery...* None of it mattered without her father in her life. Her feet touched the floor. "Mum, I'm coming as soon as I can."

"I think that's a good idea."

Her mother was always straight with her. Elena clutched her phone, squeezing her eyes shut against the anguish and rocking back and forth on the edge of her bed in the dark, unable to respond.

"Elena?"

"Tell him I'm coming. Tell him to hang on and wait for

me."

With hardly time to process what was happening to her beloved, rambunctious father, she hung up and tapped airlines sites for flights. She found a Qantas flight that left LAX within two hours. After she'd paid for the ticket online, she sank her head in her hands. He was only fifty years old. *How could this have happened?*

Acting quickly, she shoved a couple of t-shirts, a pair of jeans, and a few toiletries into a shoulder bag she used for shopping. She tapped out a short message to the women's shelter where she was due to volunteer later in the week.

Fifteen hours later, she stepped off the flight in Sydney, Australia with the small carry-on she'd hastily packed. After clearing customs, she emerged from the airport. The autumn air was mild with a tinge of crispness on her face. With anxiety tightening her chest, she hailed a cab and gave the address of the hospital where her father had been admitted. She chewed her mouth until she tasted blood.

Rushing through the corridors, the stringent smell of antiseptic assaulting her nose, she followed the directions her mother had given her. Soon, she came to his room. *Gabe Eaton*, the card read.

Tapping on the wide door, she caught her breath and opened it. "Mum? Dad?"

Her mother crossed the room on silent feet and embraced her. "He's been sleeping off and on," Honey whispered.

Elena tiptoed to her father's bedside and sat near him, watching him breathe. Like silent sentinels, monitors blinked, measuring his heartbeat, blood pressure, and other vital signs. Peeking from underneath the sheet, a thick pad of bandages surrounded his chest. She reached out and stroked his hand, noticing how tired he looked. His fingers twitched.

"I'm here, Dad." Taking care around the machines and tubes, she bent over and kissed his forehead, fighting the panicked sensation that seized her. She tried to remain calm so as not to disturb him, but it was difficult to maintain a grip on her emotions.

A trace of a smile flickered on his face, and he twitched his finger again.

Relieved that he knew she was here, Elena stroked his cheek with her hand. This time, he opened his eyes a slit. "Hey, little fairy-wren," he murmured.

Elena swallowed a sob at his nickname for her after his favorite blue bird, managing to smile and kiss his hand instead. "Hi Dad," she said softly. "I love you."

One side of his mouth lifted. His eyes fluttered closed again.

Honey touched Elena's shoulder. "He's happy you're here. Let him rest."

Elena followed her mother from the room. Standing in the hospital corridor, she fell into her mother's arms. Tears spilled onto her face as she and her mother embraced, comforting each other.

Honey brushed her hand over Elena's hair. "While you were in the air, he had bypass surgery to remove clogged arteries. The prognosis is actually good because he's always been fit. As long as he learns to behave himself."

"His diet?"

"Awful. He could always eat anything he wanted—and did—but the plaque built up inside his arteries."

"Had there been any signs?" Elena asked, trying to make sense of how it had happened.

Honey lifted a shoulder. "He'd been a little tired. But with his high energy level, he merely seemed like everyone else."

"That's Dad." She shook her head.

"He needs to rest. Let's go to the cafeteria." Honey slung her arm over Elena's shoulder, and the two woman strolled through the corridors until the smell of food guided their way.

Elena had barely slept or eaten on the plane, yet she had little appetite now. They stood in line behind doctors, nurses, and other family and friends of patients. Nothing really interested her. Her mother ordered two cups of soup and a sandwich to share. Honey wasn't hungry either.

They sat at a table overlooking a restful garden. Elena sipped a little tomato soup. As she rested her spoon, a terrible thought occurred to her.

"Oh, my God," she cried, guilt welling within her. "This is my fault. The robbery...our loss. Dad took it awfully hard, didn't he?" Shaking her head, she blinked against tears. Had this incident been the reason he'd had a heart attack?

Honey looked shocked. "Of course not," she said hurriedly, smoothing her hand over Elena's. "Please don't think that. The robbery wasn't your fault and neither is this."

"I can't help it." Elena said, scrubbing her face with her hands. "It was a chain of events and I'm the one who started it."

"This was a long time coming," Honey insisted. "And it's hereditary. His father's health is what brought us to Sydney."

"The robbery didn't help, though, did it?"

Honey shrugged. "It was a shock. But this could've happened anytime."

"Do you really think he'll come through this?"

"His father did, didn't he? Your gramps is fit now, but that's because he had a real scare. Stopped smoking, cleaned up his diet."

"Started yoga," Elena added. At seventy-five, her gramps was a regular at the health club. She'd always laughed at his skinny legs in spandex shorts, but now she understood why he was so dedicated.

Her mother clasped her hand. "We'll all get through this together. But don't expect any more burgers on the barbie unless they're vegan bean burgers."

Elena nodded and then tried another sip of her soup. "Mum, I'm so sorry about losing the diamonds."

"They're only rocks."

"But they've meant so much to our family."

Honey sighed. "Please, that's enough. Not another word about that robbery. Let the police handle it. If they recover your jewelry, then all this worry is for nothing."

"And if they don't?"

"Then we'll deal with it," Honey said with a sharp nod. "Just like we always do."

Despite the tragedies of the last forty-eight hours, Elena felt a glimmer of hope. Her mother was the one who'd always helped her find the answers in life. Not that she raced in to solve Elena's problems for her—that wasn't Honey's style—but she helped her look for creative solutions.

This time, Elena couldn't imagine how that would help, but looking across the table at her mother—a women who'd nearly lost her husband, the love of her life, just hours before—she figured if her mother could hold out hope, then she would, too.

There were far worst things in life to be than positive. And far worse situations.

9

Los Angeles, California

AFTER ELENA STORMED away from the restaurant, Jake spent a restless night thinking about her. In retrospect, he realized he had been inconsiderate. Although he hadn't planned on it, he had asked her out for dinner, and she had taken the time to get ready.

Besides that, she'd really looked amazing. So good, in fact, it had scared him. He wasn't sure if he was ready for a relationship again. If Penelope filed a claim—and he couldn't imagine that she wouldn't unless the thieves were apprehended—then Elena would be part of an investigation.

That could be a problem.

He was shaving when the phone rang.

"Good morning, darling," his mother said, her dulcet-toned voice sweeping across the phone lines. "I'm calling to confirm our lunch date for today and make sure you're not out catching bad guys."

"Today's a good day," he said, juggling his phone and razor. "I'll see you at noon."

"I'll have to go to the bank, and after lunch I'd also like to stop at a store."

"Mom, I don't have much time for shopping today."

"It will only take ten minutes, I promise."

"Where do you need to go?" He frowned at the mirror. Her ten minutes could easily stretch into an hour. Even though he owned the company, he still had appointments to keep.

"Just a little shop," she said vaguely. "See you soon."

A little before noon, Jake made his way to his mother's home. He'd been born when his mother was forty, and now at seventy-five, he was acutely aware that her time was limited. She'd beat breast cancer once—and gave generously to support cancer research—but many of her older actor friends had passed on.

Now he made a point of having a weekly lunch with her when he was in town. It was a couple of hours out of his day, but it meant so much to her. And to him.

Barbara Charles was well known around town, and although she didn't have the rabid fan base that younger stars who lived on social media had, she was still recognized and admired.

She'd been living in Beverly Hills north of Sunset Boulevard for fifty years. She knew most of the shopkeepers and their children, and she loved to stop in to say hello. He was a hometown kid, too, having graduated from Beverly Hills High School.

"Mom, I'm here," he called out as he stepped inside the white marble foyer of her home, which looked more like an upscale hotel lobby or a movie set rather than a private home. That was the Barbara Charles image, and she lived it fully.

Twin staircases curved to the second story. White sofa and chair groupings anchored collector-quality Persian rugs in the cavernous living room, and palm trees potted in antique Chinese fish pots stood on mahogany legs. An eclectic collection of paintings by friends throughout her life lined the walls. A Palm Springs watercolor by Tony Bennett, a sad clown by Red Skelton, a cubist by Picasso, and a pastoral landscape by Winston Churchill. Beyond walls of glass, the sparkling infinity pool stretched out in the ample rolling emerald grounds of the estate.

He'd grown up here, but it had looked different then, more chintz and plaid. Then came the Asian phase, then modernist decor, and now she was in what she called her white phase. She redecorated every decade or so just for the fun of it.

As Jake was studying a Hawaiian-themed painting, Barbara descended the stairs wearing a cream dress and pearls, and holding her jewelry case in her hands. "Like it? That's one of my new acquisitions," she said. "Anthony Hopkins. I just love his brilliant use of color."

"I didn't know you knew him."

"Darling, I know almost everyone, or they know me," Barbara replied, laughing. "With their art on the walls, it's like having all my friends around me." She whirled around, her hands raised to her shoulders, her twin pearl bracelets luminous in the filtered light.

Jake smiled and kissed her on the cheek. Her positive energy had kept her at the forefront of Hollywood for years. Alfred Hitchcock once said that her personality leapt from the screen. She'd been friends with everyone from Shirley Temple to Marilyn Monroe, and Oprah Winfrey to Jennifer Lawrence. Nearly every night of the week found her at a different party, art opening, or private screening.

"Let's drop off the mega-watt jewelry at the vault first," she said. She liked to keep her most expensive jewelry in the bank vault. He'd made sure her home had sophisticated security, but she had her habits. Although she had a safe in her home, a visit to the vault was a social outing for her.

After arriving at the bank, Barbara glided through the lobby, the creamy chiffon scarf wrapped around her neck fluttering behind her. Pearl-and-diamond earrings and an opera-length pearl strand complemented her outfit.

"Darling, it's wonderful to see you," she said to an immaculately dressed older gentleman who sat across the desk from a private banker. She kissed him on the cheek.

"Babs, lovely as always."

Jake caught him looking admiringly at her legs under her flowing silk dress. He suppressed a chuckle. His Mom still had her admirers.

Smiling warmly, she said, "We have to uphold our standards, don't we?"

Her own private bankers greeted her warmly, and other tellers and patrons said hello. She stopped to talk to several people, and then descended the stairway to the bank vaults on the lower level.

While she was inside a private room depositing her jewelry, Jake kept a sharp eye out. The bank tellers had been robbed many years ago, but no one had ever made it to the safety deposit boxes. Even so, he knew the risk was present. With stylists and stars returning impressive jewelry to the vaults after the Academy Awards, this would be a prime target to hit.

After she emerged, Jake drove her to one of her favorite restaurants, Spago, where they had a table reserved in the courtyard. This too, had been one of her long-time traditions, dating back to when it was the Bistro Gardens.

The chef and owner, Wolfgang Puck, stopped to greet her. She'd known him since before he'd opened his first restaurant above Sunset Boulevard. As he kissed her hand, Barbara beamed. She was in her element.

A small split of champagne was delivered to the table, and the server poured a flute for her. "I do wish you'd join me," she said as Jake raised a glass of sparkling water to her.

"I'm on duty, Mom, and someone has to be your designated driver."

"That's why I need to find another driver," she said with a sigh.

He ordered their favorite lunch, the Maine lobster salad for her and Puck's famous cold pizza with salmon, cream cheese, and caviar for himself. They had their traditions, and his mother liked it that way.

After the server left, she sipped her champagne, eyeing him over her glass. "I'm glad you always look nice when we go out. You have no idea how much that means to me. One of my friend's children met her for dinner in torn jeans and a t-shirt. Imagine! You'd never do that."

"Not to you." He knew better around Lady Barbara. She'd actually been knighted, but she'd earned the moniker among the household staff long before that.

She looked alarmed. "Not to any woman, I should hope. Not when you ask them out to dinner."

The hairs on the back of his neck bristled as he thought about last night with Elena. "If how I'm dressed makes that much of a difference to a woman, then she's not the one for me."

"Maybe that's why I don't have any grandchildren."

"Now, Mom," he said.

A hurt expression filled her eyes, and she shrugged. "If only I could have time to play with a grandchild before it's my time to go."

"Here comes the guilt. Your mother lived to be a hundred."

"My mother never had…you know."

Jake sighed. He did know, all too well. "We're all on borrowed time, Mom. I could go tomorrow."

"Even more reason." She glanced at him through half-lidded eyes. "That young woman I met, Elena, seemed awfully nice. Genuine. Talented. Why not ask her out?"

Jake sighed. She'd probably hear it from one of her friends that he had been at the Waldorf Astoria. Nothing got past her in this town. "Actually, I did."

"Really?" She clapped her hands. "You've just added ten years to my life."

"Don't get too excited. It didn't go that well."

"Why not?" Barbara looked stunned. "She's lovely, and you're…well, mostly well-mannered."

"I don't think she would've agreed with you last night."

"What did you do?"

"For starters, it wasn't exactly a date. We were going to walk to Starbucks."

"In the morning?"

"No, it was seven at night."

She narrowed her eyes. "And how was she dressed?"

"I don't know. A dark dress."

"Wool, cotton, or silk?"

He placed his hands on the table. "What is this?"

"Answer the question."

"Silk. Maybe satin. Kind of clingy." *In all the right places.*

"High heels?"

"Very." *And gorgeous legs.*

"When did you ask her out?"

When his mother frowned at him, he answered. "Earlier that day."

"And you did you say coffee or dinner?"

"Well, dinner, I guess. But I didn't specify what kind of dinner."

"Ah ha," she said triumphantly. "It *was* a date. And what did you wear?"

Jake peered around. "I think we need more water."

Drumming her manicured nails on the tablecloth, she said, "You showed up in jeans and thought you were going to pawn off coffee on her when you'd made a date? I'm *mortified.* I'm sure she was, too. You got cold feet, didn't you?"

"Mom, it wasn't like that."

"Then how was it?"

Jake drew a hand across his forehead. He'd swear his mother had a crystal ball. All his life she'd been able to extract details from people. She would've made a great attorney. Or maybe he should add her to his staff. "Pretty much like that," he admitted.

"At this rate, I'll never have…well, you know what I mean." She nodded to the server, who refilled her champagne from the small split in the ice bucket. "Are you at least going to help her find her jewelry?"

"In this case, that's a job for the police and the FBI."

"Then why were you at Penelope Plessen's house talking to her and her boyfriend yesterday?"

"How did you know…?"

"Housekeeper network. Ours are sisters."

"This town is way too small—"

"Something was said about a claim?"

"Mom, that's confidential."

"Darling, would you rather I misconstrue half the story?"

Jake lifted his gaze heavenward. "All I'm saying is that anyone who carries insurance can file a claim."

Barbara watched the bubbles in her glass in thought. "Then you'd have to investigate and establish value. You'd have to talk to Elena." Her eyes widened and she leaned forward. "That's what you were trying to do? You know, I spoke to Penelope at the party. I'll tell you right now that jewelry is the real deal." She snapped her napkin. "And so is Elena."

Jake lifted his shoulders and let them fall. He wished half the people who worked for him were as good as she was.

Fortunately, the food arrived, and the conversation turned to the film that had won Best Picture. Jake listened as his mother elucidated the fine points of the film. Not only had she acted, but she'd also directed and produced quite a few films.

After they ate, Barbara reminded Jake of his promise to

take her by a shop. He collected his Jaguar from the valet attendant, and then turned onto Wilshire Boulevard. As he neared Robertson, his mother instructed him to turn.

"There's a space," she said, pointing to a vacant spot near Elena's shop.

Dutifully, he parked and helped her from the car. Walking toward Elena's shop, his mother's plan became evident.

He shook his head, amused at her, yet dreading Elena's reaction. *I deserve this.* As they drew closer, he saw the dark blue velvet drapes at the front windows were drawn.

"Why, it's closed," Barbara said, slowing her pace. "That's odd. I wonder if she's okay."

"Can I help you?" A voice with a slight Irish accent rang out behind them.

Jake turned. "We were looking for—wait, we met at the party didn't we?"

The tall redhead in a lime green dress inclined her head. "Not officially. I'm Fianna Fitzgerald."

Barbara pushed past him. "Fianna, darling. The dress you designed for Penelope was utterly gorgeous. Masterful. Aimee couldn't stop raving, told everyone at the Governor's Ball. I've been meaning to call you about a few summer frocks. And of course, I simply had to visit Elena. I really want to see her work."

Jake shook his head. Was there anyone his mother didn't know?

"She'll be sorry she missed you both," Fianna said, worry creasing her face. "She took off for Sydney late last night."

Jake jerked his head up. "In *Australia?*"

Fianna slid a glance toward Jake. "Last time I checked."

He ran his hands over the slight stubble that was already appearing on his jawline. Elena had just fled the country. *Not a good sign.* He touched his mother's arm. "Mom, it's time to go." Remembering his manners, he added, "Fianna, it was nice meeting you."

Before his mother could protest, he steered her back to the car.

Once inside, Barbara sighed and said, "Mission aborted. We'll just have to try again when she returns."

Driving north toward Sunset, he said, "Mom, you always see the best in people. But I've learned they're not always what they seem."

"Sweetheart, I know that. I can spot an actor a mile away."

That's just it. As far as he was concerned, Elena wasn't acting. This trip proved she was *actually* what he suspected. He knew insurance fraud in his gut when he saw it, and he'd never been wrong yet.

Shane Wallace came to mind. There may have been accomplices in the robbery, too. The puzzle was taking shape. He made a note to call his buddy on the force after he took his mother home. In fact, he had several calls to make.

Jake had another idea, too. Australia had a bilateral

extradition treaty with the U.S. He'd had to chase more than one criminal who'd fled the country.

But never one as intriguing and lovely as Elena.

If only the situation were different...

10

Sydney, Australia

OUTSIDE HER PARENTS' window, the morning sun streamed in. Elena could hear the ocean's incessant, rhythmic roar, as if marking the endless, interminable hours she'd spent by her father's bed. Since he'd been released from the hospital, she'd insisted on helping him eat, dress, and walk.

She didn't mind. This was her penance for having been so far away when her beloved father's heart failed him. *What if Dad hadn't made it?* She would have never forgiven herself. She sat by her father's bed now, reading as he slept.

A seagull squawked outside and Elena looked out. She had grown up here in the beach cottage. Before returning to her book, she glanced around, appreciating the familiarity of her surroundings. Wood floors were worn smooth by sand tracked inside, and white canvas slipcovers her mother regularly bleached still covered worn chairs. On the wall hung shadowboxes filled with shells she'd made for her mum one

Mother's Day.

She inhaled deeply. The scent of the ocean permeated everything.

"Finished with breakfast?" Her mother entered, strolling in wearing jeans and a nubby sweater looped around her neck over a t-shirt. Her short brown hair was a few shades lighter than Elena's, and people often mistook them for sisters. She brushed it from her forehead and tucked it behind her ears.

Elena nodded and lowered her book. "Have a good run?"

"I did."

Her mother swam in the ocean or ran nearly every morning. Elena favored her in her build, and she knew her father had always liked her mother's curvy figure. *You look fine in a bikini, Honey,* he'd often say. As Elena matured into a teenager, her mother had given her confidence about her body image. She'd been the first one in her class to grow breasts, and she'd been embarrassed about being top heavy.

Her mother rested a hand on Elena's shoulder, so Elena slid a tattered bookmark into her old copy of *My Brilliant Career.* At her mother's gesture, she followed her from her parents' room.

Honey faced her. "He's out of danger, but I'm worried about you now." Her mother nodded toward the old book Elena held. "Reading that again?"

"Wild horses or waves, writing or jewelry-making, it's all about the same, isn't it?"

"What do you mean?"

"I've been thinking about the choices we make in life, or as women, the choices that are made for us." As she'd worked on the necklace she'd made for Penelope to wear, she treated each diamond with care, knowing what they had once meant to someone. *Freedom. Security. A future.*

Her mother shot a concerned look her way. "Interesting you say that."

With the book clasped to her chest, Elena strolled through the cottage and stepped outside, where the sea mist was moist on her face and the autumn breeze mild. The temperature was similar to that of Southern California, with the seasons reversed.

She sank into a chair on the porch overlooking the beach from a distance, where people rode or paddled on boards in the sea, lounged on the beach, or walked the shoreline. Other brave souls took turns leaping off a large flat rock while a brigade of surf lifesavers—the first such club in the world years ago—kept an eye on everyone. Her parents had lived here for years, but in today's market, this was an expensive view.

Honey sat beside her, cupping her chin in her hand as she gazed out to sea. "We've always tried to give you the freedom to do what you wanted to in life."

"As it turns out, that includes the freedom to make enormous mistakes." Elena drew her legs up and clasped her knees. She wore soft blue jeans and a t-shirt, which outside of a swimsuit, is what she'd gown up in on the beach. She rested her chin on her knees. "Adulting is hard work, Mum."

Honey laughed. "Of course it is, especially when—or if—you marry and have children."

Elena reached over and clasped her mother's hand. "Thanks for never pressuring me about that."

"You've always had your own mind. I trust you to make the right decisions."

Elena winced. "I really blew it this time, didn't I?" Perhaps she'd bit off too much in L.A. and wasn't cut out for the big time. Not everyone was.

"Things happen outside of our control. You took a gamble, that's all. Most everyone who's been successful has had a few missteps along the way."

"This robbery gave me perspective about the one thing that's really important in life. You and Dad...how could I have been so selfish as to leave you here on your own?"

Honey laughed softly. "I might be sitting in a rocking chair, but I'm not as old as you think."

"But Dad—"

"Hit a bad spell, that's all," she said firmly. "Not saying it wasn't a close call, but with good doctors, fine care, and taking better care of himself, he'll be fine. Don't worry."

"Maybe I should plan on staying close to home." As near as Elena could tell, unless her jewelry was recovered, she'd have to revise her life anyway. She'd fled L.A. to be near her father, but now that she was here, she was seriously thinking of staying. The robbery had really plunged her into a depression. Now she was doubting her ability to bounce back.

"My apartment in L.A., my shop—they're expensive overhead, and now that I've bankrupted you—"

"Stop it. You haven't." Her mother waved a hand, gesturing at the beach community. "Look at where we're living. This piece of land is our retirement, but we've got a long way to go before that happens. As for you...we bet on you and we'd do it again. We're not feeble old folks, so stop treating us that way. Fifty is the new thirty, or haven't you heard?"

"You've always looked good for your age. We're even the same size still." Elena had packed so little in such a hurry when she left that she'd been wearing her mother's clothes. Honey ran a trendy beach boutique not far from her dad's surf school and rentals.

"And your dad just got a tune-up. So don't use us as an excuse to come limping home when the first bad break comes along."

How had her mother suspected? Elena's mouth dropped open. "I'm not—"

"Are you sure? The girl I raised couldn't wait to show the world what she could do. You were always different, Elena. Always had a grand plan. Never meant for this lazy beach scene. You know that in your heart, and you have a real talent."

As if mocking Elena, the sound of laughing kookaburra birds erupted from nearby trees. She craned her neck and shaded her eyes. Raising her voice, she cried, "Knock it off up there."

More cackles sounded as the birds took flight.

Honey pursed her lips. "Those diamonds led you to what you were meant to do."

"They're gone now." Blinking hard, she averted her eyes toward the breaking waves, catching sight of seagulls soaring over the ocean. She remembered the thrill she'd felt as a little girl the first time she'd ever seen the unusual stones.

"Look at me, Elena."

She sighed and turned back to her mother, who stared at her with a fierce expression that she knew all too well.

"The stones aren't gone," Honey said. "They're just somewhere else at the moment. Maybe they'll be returned. Or not. Regardless, you have to move on."

"But they were so special…"

Her mother's face softened as she held her hand to the sunlight, admiring the wedding ring she wore—a precious blue diamond that reflected the brilliance of the sea. "Yes, but they were always sort of bewitched. They go where they're needed."

At lunch time the house phone rang, and Elena answered it. "We've got tickets for *Madame Butterfly*," Elena's grandfather told her. "Dress up and meet us at the opera house," he insisted, telling her where and when.

Before Elena could argue, Gramps hung up. She shook her head. When people called her uncompromising, at least she knew where she got it from.

Whether her mother was behind this or not, she didn't know, but as the afternoon wore on she found herself looking forward to going. The opera house was one of her favorite spots in Sydney. With its stunning architectural rendering reminiscent of billowing white sails juxtaposed against crystal blue harbor waters, it was a sight to behold.

Now in their seventies, Elena's paternal grandparents, known as Grams and Gramps since she'd been a little girl, had long been involved in Sydney's social scene. They'd both been active in real estate sales and development in the Sydney harbor area for years, and had funded a private center for abused women. Now they had a condo in Rushcutters Bay, a popular neighborhood.

They had worked hard for their retirement, earning every bit of the life they now enjoyed and still exploring the world as they had in their youth.

As Elena shimmied into an ebony silk dress of her mother's—the only black item in Honey's closet she could find—she recalled the fun she'd had with them over the years. A culinary trip to San Francisco, skiing in Lake Tahoe, a wine-tasting trip to Napa, and a visit to the Grand Canyon on still another excursion.

Considering the life they led, Elena thought of her

mother's words. She had to believe that seventy was also the new fifty. Between yoga, tai chi, and Pilates, they had active lives. Every year they visited her in the United States, took a personal vacation somewhere, and spent two weeks in India on charitable missions. Seeing them gave her hope for her father.

She slipped into a pair of her mother's lower-heeled shoes and turned to the mirror in her parents' dressing area.

"Where's my fairy-wren? Come let me see you," her father called.

Elena stepped out and twirled around, feeling as she had as a child. In fact, being here made her feel like she had retreated to her childhood. As much as she loved her family, she was beginning to understand her mother's admonition. Maybe she was using this excuse to hide from her problems in L.A.

Her father's eyes lit up and he grinned. "You're as beautiful as your mother in that dress, and that's the highest compliment I can give you."

Honey leaned against the door jamb. "I should hope so."

"You know what would look smashing with that?" Without waiting for an answer, her dad continued. "The hammered silver collar necklace you made for your mum."

Honey retrieved it from a drawer and slipped it around Elena's neck. "I love it. Perfect for tonight."

Elena kissed them both, then ran out the door to meet her grandparents.

The senior Eatons, Lana and Aaron, were well-known in the vibrant arts community and as soon as Elena arrived, they introduced her to several of their friends outside the opera house. They were an attractive, silver-haired couple who had an ease and grace about them that drew others to them.

She'd always thought Grams was particularly stunning. With her deep olive complexion, which Elena had inherited, she tanned quickly in the Sydney sunshine, and with her styled white hair and regal posture, she was simply striking.

Chatting with her grandparents' friends outside the magnificent structure perched on Bennelong Point, a peninsula near one of the world's widest long-span bridges, the Sydney Harbour Bridge, Elena stood in awe of the dazzling light display projected on the side of the soaring, white sail-themed roof of the opera house. A spectacular, brilliantly-colored animation splashed across the arched tiled roof.

Grams smiled at her. "I wanted you to see this new First Nations animated film. It's called Badu Gigli, which means 'water light' in the Gadigal language."

"It's impressive." Elena watched the animation, luminous against the night sky, as native Australian birds soared across the sails, frogs scampered from lily pads, and fish swam through waves. Images of the harbors and mountains, bush and outback, and native artifacts were vividly rendered in a tribute to Australian history. Elena was filled with pride for her family's homeland as she watched the artistry unfold in radiant splendor, illuminating the evening.

After a few minutes, it ended, and Elena kissed her grandmother on the cheek. "Thanks for bringing me tonight, Grams."

"Life is for the living, dear. Gabe is going to be fine, so it's time you got out."

"Just have to limit his barbecued ribs, aye?" her grandfather said, chuckling. "We'll make him vegan yet. Or at least a pescetarian."

Elena smiled at the thought of her dad, a proud master griller, changing his ways. But she knew her mother would be adamant about modifying his diet. "I'm glad you broke me out of the house after all."

Taking in the sparkling city lights surrounding the harbor and the twinkling lights on boats cruising the waterway, Elena felt a measure of happiness. More than that, she was so relieved that her father had made progress with his health.

"It's so gorgeous here," she said. With her eyes on the lights, she spun around, taking in the glittering treasure of Sydney. Behind her, her grandparents laughed at her delight.

As she twirled to a stop, a figure in the distance caught her attention. At nighttime, it was hard to see. She looked closer.

Startled to see someone who seemed familiar, she squinted, but the gathering crowd obscured her vision. She shuddered the thought away. *That's impossible.*

Turning back to her grandmother, she asked, "Were you able to find good seats this late?"

"We have season tickets next to friends of ours," her grandmother replied. "So if they can't make a performance, or we can't, we can invite others. Works well for us."

Elena's grandmother was as pragmatic as her mother. She looked over her shoulder again, disturbed at the similarity she saw in the man who was now approaching the entry. She swung back to her grandparents. "Let's go in."

"Wait," Gramps said. "We should take a photo here in front with the opera house in the background. A selfie—isn't that what you call it? To show your friends in America."

"Elena?" A man called out behind them.

At the sound of Jake's voice, Elena clenched her jaw. *How can this be?*

11

DESPITE THE COOL evening, Elena's neck burned with anger as Jake made his way toward her across the expanse in front of the Sydney Opera House.

"Perfect," Gramps said. "Look, here's someone you know. He can take it." He motioned to Jake.

There was no avoiding him.

"Elena!"

As Jake's voice rang out, she wished she could dive into the ocean lapping around the peninsula on which the opera house was situated.

Her grandfather handed his phone to Jake. "We were just taking a photograph before we went in. Would you mind? Ta."

Gramps hugged Elena and Grams to his sides with a broad smile as Jake centered them in the frame.

Elena faked a smile. After Jake snapped the photo and returned the phone to Gramps, she said, "What are you doing here?"

"I'm as surprised as you are." Jake's gaze traveled up the opera house. "That animation was incredibly well done. I love seeing this, don't you?"

"You're from America," Gramps said, introducing themselves. "A friend of Elena's from Los Angeles, I presume."

"You'd be correct, sir," he said, shaking her grandfather's hand with a solid grip.

"My, what a small world," Grams said. "Your friend coming here on the same evening. Imagine that."

Grams swung a questioning look to Elena, who was concentrating on sinking through the concrete slab beneath them, or making a run for it. Instead, she said, "Yes, how strange."

"I just stopped by to see the place. I hadn't planned on going to the opera."

Elena said, "He doesn't like opera."

"Actually, I'm a huge fan."

"*Madame Butterfly* is on tonight," Gramps offered. "No ticket, no worries. We have an extra, mate."

"No," Elena cried, though she knew how rude that sounded.

"Thank you, sir, I'd like that very much," Jake replied.

Gramps shot a stern look at Elena. "No trouble at all. He's a guest in our country and enjoys opera. What could be better?"

Besides a slow death by torture? Elena glared at Jake.

"He insists on paying for the ticket, don't you?"

"Elena, don't be silly," Grams said, laughing. "We're happy to host this fine, opera-loving young lad. Shall we go in?"

Jake offered his arm to Elena, and she sent him a withering look. *How can this be?* She was going to be seated next to him for *hours.*

"Just kill me now," she muttered under her breath, praying for a lightning bolt as they crossed to enter. Ideally, it would strike him, but she'd take it, too.

No such luck. They went inside.

In the darkened theater, as the house in Nagasaki, Japan loomed on the stage and Pinkerton and Butterfly enacted their love on the soaring notes of "Bimba, Bimba, non piangere" on stage, Elena leaned toward Jake and whispered. "Are you clueless or utterly insane?"

"I'm not the one who fled to Sydney," Jake replied calmly.

"*Fled?*" Elena was incensed. "My father could have *died.*"

The man on the other side of her raised a finger to his lips for silence and whispered, "*Tutti ziti.*"

The significance wasn't lost on her. *Quiet everyone.* It was a song in the performance, too.

Jake nodded. "We need to talk later."

"I have absolutely nothing to say to you."

"I can make this easy on you."

"What are you talking about?" Elena whispered loudly, gesturing. A woman in front of her turned around.

This time, Grams shot her a reprimanding look.

Elena crossed her arms and stared ahead. After a while, even though she'd seen the opera before, she forgot her animosity and became immersed in the story. The exquisite music soared into her soul, while the artistry of the performers mesmerized her. The elaborate costumes and set combined to sweep her into a magical realm.

At intermission, Jake touched her hand, breaking the spell she'd been under. "Elena, I just have questions about the origin of your stones."

Elena snapped her hand back. "This is not the time or place, and even if it were—"

Standing, Grams turned to them. "Let's have a stretch. Come on, you two."

As soon as they cleared the theater, Elena shot to the ladies room. Thankfully, there was already a long line.

"There you are. We lost you in the crowd." Grams said, the folds of her white silk dress fluttering as she approached her.

"Sorry, thought I'd grab a spot in line."

Grams smiled at her. "My goodness, Jake seems nice. So well mannered."

"You haven't known him very long."

Surprise crossed Gram's smooth face. "He said he just met you. And he's crazy about you."

Now it was Elena's turn to be surprised. "He said that?"

"Didn't have to. The way he looks at you, it's obvious."

Elena shook her head. "Grams, no offense, but you're seriously out of touch."

Her grandmother laughed. "Can't imagine young people are falling in love much differently today than we did."

"Oh, no. No, no, no." Elena folded her arms. "That's the last thing on his mind, believe me. All he wants is the diamonds."

"Well, isn't that what you want, too, dear?" Grams smoothed her hand around Elena's shoulders, just as she'd done when Elena was a young girl. "He said he was investigating the disappearance. Seems like someone you'd want on your side."

The line snaked forward. As it did, another woman said hello to her grandmother. Elena tried to act sociable, as she knew Grams would want, but Jake's presence gnawed at her.

When they returned, Elena changed the seating order. "I want to sit between you two," she said to her grandparents. "I don't see enough of you." She took their hands in each of hers. It was either that or she was going to feign an upset stomach and leave, but knowing her grandparents, they'd either leave with her, or worse, dispatch Jake to see her home.

Jake took the change gamely and sat next to her grandfather, whom she was certain would test Jake's knowledge on opera.

She didn't have to wait long.

"We often go to the opera when we visit Los Angeles, too," Gramps said. "What have been your favorite performances there?"

Now he'll be discovered. Elena folded her arms, even more satisfied with her plan.

"Besides the obvious, *Carmen, Don Giovanni, Rigoletto…*" Jake began. "A few years ago, John Corigliano wrote music for *The Ghosts of Versailles,* the first major U.S. staging of that work in two decades. It was amazing. Renée Fleming sang, and she was also in Andre Previn's *A Streetcar Named Desire.*" Jake leaned forward to include Elena in the conversation. "My mother is a founder of the Los Angeles Music Center, and I often go with her to opera performances at the Dorothy Chandler Pavilion."

To her dismay, Jake was a true aficionado. If only he'd been that engaging on their first non-date. However, now the game had clearly changed. Why was he here, and why was he so interested in her jewelry? Her mind whirred as the lights dimmed for the next act.

After the performance was over, Jake followed her outside. While her grandparents greeted other people, Jake turned to her.

"That was nice of your grandparents to include me."

"My grandparents are kind people."

Jake watched them mingle with other people. "They seem well known."

"They've supported the arts here for years," Elena said thoughtfully. "They're not L.A. super-wealthy, but they've helped a lot of people buy first homes and send their kids to better schools. They believe in helping people. So do my parents." That's why they'd all agreed that she should use the diamonds in her work to create a lasting legacy.

Jake considered her words. "I'm sorry about the other night," he said, his voice earnest. "I'm sure a lot of guys get nervous around you."

"Nervous? What for?"

He was quiet for a moment, his eyes reflecting the glittering harbor lights. "You can be a little intimidating."

"You can do better than that."

"Look in the mirror lately?"

"Right," Elena replied, rolling her eyes. "Get to the point about what you said about my diamonds in there. Have they been found?"

A smile flickered across his face, then disappeared. "No, but Penelope didn't want you to suffer a loss. Since she'd taken responsibility of your jewelry, she filed an insurance claim under her policy."

"Oh. I see." Elena shivered in the cool breeze off the water and wrapped her arms around herself. *Maybe I should try to be civil in this matter.* Instead of looking at his velvety brown eyes, she gazed across the harbor. "Does that mean all hope of recovery is gone?"

"The investigation is still open, and the police and FBI

are following up on leads. However, the more time that passes, the lower the chance of recovery."

Elena knew that. She also knew that the jewelry might've been smuggled from the country and sold into another market. Or the gemstones removed and used in other settings. She sighed. "You mean my work of art is being parted out like a stolen car."

"It's possible."

Elena blinked into the wind, struggling to come to grasp with reality. She'd put so much love and labor into the pieces, it broke her heart to know the only thing some people valued was the cost of the materials.

To her, jewelry was art, and she derived satisfaction from knowing a woman was wearing her work and enjoying it. She loved the idea that a piece she created would be lovingly passed on to a woman's daughter or those she loved.

Just as her grandmother and great-grandmother had with Sabeena's diamonds. And her heartbreaking story.

"The insurance company will pay the claim after it's satisfied that the jewelry won't be recovered. Isn't that good news?"

"I suppose so." That meant she'd be able to keep her salon and continue working. Otherwise, she could be bankrupt. It was a consolation, but it wasn't the only reason she'd taken on the risk and toiled so hard.

Jake waited a beat. "I want to help you. I'm sure you could use the money, right?"

"It isn't just about the money." Her dream had been to create something of beauty to share with the world so she could continue doing what she loved. What she'd been fated to do. Because it was fate that had delivered the diamonds to her.

"Okay. Making a name for yourself is important, right? A lot of photos were taken of Penelope. You've received a lot of publicity."

Elena lifted a corner of her mouth. There was that at least. "That helps."

"You probably got even more exposure than if the robbery hadn't occurred." Jake threw a glance over his shoulder at her grandparents, who were still visiting with friends. "The theft got you mentioned in the same breath as all the greats. Cartier, Bulgari, Harry Winston."

"Sure, but…" How could she make him understand how deeply the process of creation was ingrained in her? What this really meant to her? She wanted to fulfill a dream for her ancestors, for the women who had suffered to provide a better life for her.

"You might never have been recognized on such a level."

Elena took a step back. "Are you saying I'm not talented enough to be recognized alongside them?" It wasn't all about being on the world stage. She glanced back at the opera house, singular in its magnificence. She was also driven by her passion for excellence and her innate need to create beauty, as other artists were.

"I didn't say that." Jake rocked on his feet. "In fact, your work is astounding. I've been inspecting photos, and I saw your work at your salon. You're talented, Elena. I mean it."

"Then why are you here? Why couldn't you have called or emailed?"

"I needed to talk to you in person." Jake drew his hand across his forehead. "You see, the insurance company won't pay out unless they're satisfied the loss is real."

"*Real?* This is about as real as it gets. You have no idea what I've been through."

"That's not what they mean." Jake glanced at her grandparents again. "The diamonds. They're extremely rare. They want to know where you purchased them. They need documentation. Receipts."

"They are real, I assure you." Elena pursed her lips and swung away from him. That was the one thing she couldn't help him with. "All I can give you is my word."

12

STEPPING INTO THE cabin cruiser moored at Rushcutters Bay in a bustling yacht club, Jake couldn't help but enjoy the view around him. However, the best view of all was that of Elena, who had gone aboard before him. She wore a pair of slim white jeans, deck shoes, and a French blue-and-white striped sweater.

Last night at the opera, Elena's grandmother had sweetly asked him to join them on a harbor cruise today. She was in the galley preparing fresh fruits and vegetables she'd brought on board for hors d'oeuvres, while her husband Aaron steered from the slip. Elena had immediately gone below to help Lana.

Once they were outside of the marina and into the harbor, Aaron picked up speed. Jake stood at the bow of the cabin cruiser as it coursed through the harbor waters, while the city of Sydney rose around him. Tilting his chin into the wind, he felt the cool ocean spray mist his face.

He'd quickly accepted Lana's invitation for today, even

though he knew Elena would be upset. This was purely business, he told himself. Glancing behind him, he saw Elena on the bridge, taking over from her grandfather while he chatted on the phone. Still, he couldn't help the physical longing he felt for her. But that's all it was, he told himself. She wanted nothing to do with him, right?

As soon as Penelope had filed the claim, his buddy at her insurance company told him to start the investigation. The leads the police and FBI were following had grown cold, but they held out hope. However, the insurance company had a limited time in which to respond to the claim.

He'd planned to gather as much information as he could here while he waited for an arrest warrant to be issued in the States—if he could prove the potential of fraud. The District Attorney needed a lot more to go on than what he had. Just having a suspicion of fraud was not enough. He needed something more.

Having been an instrumental part of teams that had brought jewel thieves and insurance fraud perpetrators to justice, he'd performed this task before. However, he'd never met anyone quite like Elena, and he found it disconcerting.

What he couldn't figure was why would a young woman like her, who had so much going for her, risk it all for a quick hit that could ruin her brilliant future? She'd studied hard to get where she was, didn't live extravagantly, and didn't seem to have any bad habits he could see—those always left trails.

He'd received a clean report on her from another

investigator just this morning. No evidence of gambling, drugs, extortion, or anything else people got involved in.

Furthermore, now that he had met her grandparents, who were fine people, doubt was creeping into his mind. While he had nabbed his share of white-collar criminals, in his experience the Elena that was emerging no longer fit the profile.

Or was that what he wanted to believe?

All he wanted was for her to tell him the truth about the gemstones, but she'd refused. If only he'd treated her better from the beginning. He'd been guilty of exactly what his mother had accused him of.

You have approach avoidance, his mother had charged. *Whatever.* He glanced at Elena again, feeling a quickening of his heart.

"How about a champagne toast to christen the cruise?" Lana carried two flutes and handed one to him before he could contest. "To new friends," she said, clinking his plastic flute.

"*Salut*," he said. Lana was an interesting woman who was passionate about opera, spoke with knowledge about real estate, and had traveled the world. He saw traces of Lana in Elena's face and imagined that Elena would age just as gracefully.

Where did that thought come from?

Perturbed, he took a sip of champagne. As he did, his eyes were drawn to a necklace Lana wore. "What an interesting piece," he said.

"Elena designed this for me. Reset the stone in platinum. It was one of her earlier works." She touched it with reverence. "I just love it; it's special." A smile played on her face, and she glanced back at Aaron. "It's been quite lucky for me."

Curious, he looked closer. "That's a blue diamond, isn't it?"

"Not quite the size of the Hope, but it's unique."

"Very." He chose his words with care. "Fancy-colored diamonds are my favorites because they're so rare."

Lana arched an eyebrow. "Funny they didn't have much value—unless they were exceedingly large—until more recently. Brilliant whites dominated the market and were the favored gemstones in India among the elite for centuries." She paused. "Did you see the diamonds Penelope wore?"

"Not up close, but I've seen photos." His interest piqued, he asked, "Is that stone from Australia? The Argyle mine has produced some fine colored blue diamonds. Though mostly pink, brown, and champagne. Even a few red and purple diamonds."

"Like the Blue Moon." Lana smiled. "No, it's not from the outback."

He guessed again. "The Cullinan mine in South Africa?"

Lana's dark brown eyes twinkled. "No dear, this has a much longer history than that. This has been in the family for—"

"What are you doing?" Elena appeared behind them, glaring at Jake.

Jake swung around, but before he could answer, Lana said, "He was admiring my necklace, dear."

Elena shot him a look that could flatten champagne bubbles. "And wanting to know where the diamond came from?" She turned to leave.

Jake caught her hand, intrigued by this new information. "Were the gemstones in Penelope's jewelry from your family?"

Elena exchanged a furtive glance with her grandmother. "Why should it matter? I know what I had. I just can't prove it to your lawyers."

"If you tell me about it, maybe I can help." This isn't what the insurance adjuster would want to hear, but he felt he had a duty to Elena, too. If these were part of an inheritance, then this could be a true loss. Again, documentation would help.

Lana gave Elena a nearly imperceptible nod.

What's that about? he wondered briefly.

Elena glared at him. "India."

His lips parted. Some of the most coveted diamonds came from India, where stones had been mined longer than on other continents. "Of course," he said, half to himself. "Legendary diamonds...the blue Wittelsbach-Graff is from the Kollur mines in Andhra Pradesh, as are the Koh-i-noor and Regent diamonds, which are perfectly white and flawless."

Elena nodded. "The Great Mogul and the Orlov diamonds, too."

"And probably the Hope diamond," Lana added, her eyes sparkling. "From the sixteen hundreds, at least."

Elena gazed ahead at the ocean as she spoke, her eyes as blue as the wide sky above and the diamond around Lana's neck. "Diamonds were found along the Krishna River from the Kollur Mine to Paritala as far back as the fourth century B.C., and maybe longer."

"Are these…?"

"Mostly, yes," she said simply.

Jake narrowed his eyes. "Then how did you come by them?"

Lana and Elena exchanged glances. Finally, Elena said, "You're awfully good at finding the guilty people. Trouble is, you've forgotten how to recognize the innocent ones."

Jake grew quiet. She had a point. Had he become so guarded and suspicious of people that he could no longer open his heart? He pressed his lips together and stared from the bow, trying to recall the last time he'd let a woman in without vetting her first.

He couldn't.

Elena leaned on the railing next to him, and Lana left to check on Aaron. "Ever wondered what makes a diamond blue?" she asked, the breeze from the Sydney harbor whipping her hair from her forehead. She closed her eyes and arched the length of her neck.

Taking in her profile, Jake was reminded of beautiful nautical figureheads at the bows of ships. Unable to help himself, he slid his arm next to hers. The slight touch zapped his synapses, and he swallowed hard. Dragging his attention back to her question, he said, "Boron, I believe."

"That's right." A smile playing on her lips, she turned to him. "Not many know it only takes a trace of boron during formation to absorb red light, which turns the diamond blue, along with low nitrogen content. It's a freak of nature, actually." She paused. "So you'll probably want to test the stones."

Jake nodded. "I have lab experts I'll engage."

"You can test the diamond in my necklace. I still have a few smaller stones, too."

"And the green diamonds?"

"I traded some blues for greens." She gazed out to sea again. "So if they pass, will you start believing me?"

Jake slid his hand over hers. The probability of mixing authentic diamonds with faux stones was slim, but he'd seen it done where large, valuable center stones were replaced. In the high stakes gamble of insurance fraud, he'd seen everything.

It didn't mean that she would be in the clear, but a positive test would help swing the pendulum in her direction. He still needed more to convince the insurance company. Anything she could prove or tell him would help.

Yet that wasn't all he needed—or wanted.

He looked down at their joined hands.

Lacing his fingers with Elena's, he was surprised and pleased to see her responding in kind. He could feel his heart pounding; to his ears it was so thunderous he wondered if she could hear it. Further, he knew he was treading in delicate territory with her emotions.

Summoning his courage, he said, "Would you like to join me for dinner? This time, I promise a proper date, high heels and all."

"Lucky you. I left them all in L.A."

He folded her hand in his. "Aaron told me about your father. I realize this is important family time, and I don't mean to take you away from him."

Elena tipped her head. "Fortunately, he's making tremendous improvement. My parents have accused me of hovering. They've been kicking me out of the house every chance they get." She smiled. "So yes, I'll take you up on that very decent offer."

Jake caressed her hand. "Would it be too much to ask you to tell me the story of the stones?"

Elena shot a look back toward her grandmother, who was standing beside her husband. "I'll see," she said. "It's not entirely up to me."

After cruising the harbor, Aaron and Lana suggested they have dinner at Doyle's on the beach, a Sydney restaurant that had been on the same spot in Watson's Bay for more than a hundred years.

"It's an institution," Aaron said, pride evident in his voice.

Jake was enjoying talking to Aaron. Since Barbara had been much younger than his father, he'd hardly known his dad and often wished he'd had the chance to have a relationship with him as an adult. Maybe it would have helped him understand women better.

Once they reached Watson's Bay, Aaron pulled alongside a pier and they disembarked.

As they made their way to Doyle's, Jake remarked, "What a fantastic lifestyle you have in Sydney. Everything seems so relaxed."

"We like it," Aaron said with a wink. "Sydney's a unique place, but the fact is, you can enjoy life just about anywhere as long you make your mind up to it."

They sat outside overlooking the bay, surrounded by the laughter of people having a good time. Without a doubt, Sydney had crept under his skin.

They dined on mussels and calamari, shrimp and crab, and heaps of fresh vegetables and salads, which was most of what Aaron ate, he noticed.

Jake kept slipping glances at Elena throughout dinner, and she did the same. He was certain that Lana and Aaron caught them, too, but hadn't they encouraged him at the opera? In the space of just two days, his entire mission to Sydney had changed.

And it scared the hell out of him.

Lifting his glass of sauvignon blanc, he drank in the delicate flavor. Lana was staring at him with her dark brown eyes and a look of expectation on her face.

Seizing the opportunity, he cleared his throat and asked, "What's the story behind the blue diamonds?"

Elena quickly glanced at her grandmother.

At first, no one answered. Then Aaron slid his hand into his wife's and leaned over to kiss her cheek. "That's a family secret, mate."

And one that Jake vowed to learn.

13

THE NEXT MORNING, Elena awoke to bright sunshine. Autumn weather in Sydney was mild, so she'd planned to go for a morning walk on the beach. She loved this time of year at the beach—there were fewer tourists, and it was quieter and less crowded.

Honey came into her room as Elena was lacing up her shoes. She'd already made breakfast for her parents, who were early risers, and spent time with her dad playfully arguing over a crossword puzzle in the morning paper.

"Going for a walk?" Honey peered from the window. "Don't dawdle, I hear a storm is moving in later."

"What's a little rain?" Elena plunged her arms into a windbreaker.

"You'll need your sunnies for now, but should be a big one."

Elena pushed her sunglasses on top of her head. She'd started for the front door when she heard a knock. "Expecting someone?"

Approaching the door, she was surprised to see Jake through the screen. He was wearing shorts and a sweatshirt and looked awfully good. *Great legs*, she thought, casually noting his muscular calves.

He grinned when he saw her. "Wanted to say good morning. Lana told me where you lived."

"It's my parents' place."

"Hope I'm not too early. She said you'd all be up at the crack of dawn and that I should stop by."

"That's Grams." She smiled and leaned against the doorjamb. "I was just going for a walk. Want to join me?"

"Sure. I've never seen Bondi Beach."

"So, is this Jake?" Honey appeared behind her.

Elena wondered how much Grams had told her. She introduced them, and they chatted for a few minutes before her mother invited him inside.

"Come meet Gabe," Honey said, guiding him into a sun-filled room adjoining the kitchen where Gabe was spending a lot of time during his recovery.

"Awfully glad to meet you. Heard a lot about you," Gabe said.

Not from me, Elena thought but said nothing. Grams must have been filling in her parents. She folded her arms and watched in amusement as her parents peppered Jake with questions as if they were dating. He handled them all with easy banter.

Elena leaned against the door jamb. *Dating? Maybe I've*

agreed to one *date*. Now that she was finally getting to know him, she sort of hoped it wouldn't be their last. He seemed a lot less abrasive than when they'd first met.

But should she trust him yet? Or was he still merely trying to find out information about her for the insurance claim?

Her parents were still asking questions, so Elena finally cut in, laughing. "That's enough. Poor Jake probably hasn't even had his morning coffee yet."

As she pulled him through the hall, she glanced back at her mother, who was silently clapping with glee.

Mothers.

Once outside, Jake said, "Your parents seem nice. I really enjoyed meeting them."

"We get along well now," Elena said, heading toward the beach. "I was a pretty feisty teenager, but they saw me through it." She grinned, kicking up sand as they jogged down to the beach. A few surfers were coming in on waves. She wondered if she knew any of them, though it had been a couple of years since she'd surfed here. Preferring to wait for her dad, she'd decided not to surf on this trip. "I spent too much time on surfboards and not enough on books. Dated too many surfers…that sort of thing."

"Hmm. Like Shane Wallace?"

Elena stopped. "Why do you ask about him? Do you even know him?"

"He was at Bow-Tie that night," Jake said, looking a

little guilty for bringing up his name. "I saw you talking with him."

"If you're still investigating me," she said, putting a hand on her hip. "Then you can leave right now. I don't care how busy Grams and Gramps have been putting us in each other's way."

"Point taken." He looked truly regretful. "I didn't mean it the way it sounded."

She reached for his hand. "Can we not talk about the robbery for just one day? All I've done is think about the loss and what it means to me and my family. I could use a break before I have to go back to L.A. and face it." The stress of the robbery and her father's condition had frazzled her nerves. She really needed a day of respite.

"I'd like that, too." Jake stretched his well-defined arm across her shoulder and watched the sets of waves coming in. "Tell me more about Bondi Beach. What was it like to grow up here?"

"Pretty great, I have to say." The feeling of his arm warmed her, and she leaned easily into him. She went on to tell him about how she learned to surf and the Australian tradition of celebrating a second Christmas in July with a winter fest. Pointing, she added, "That's where the ice skating rink is set up for winter fest."

Jake laughed. "Ice skating with a beach view. Now that's interesting." He nodded toward a rock swimming pool built into the sea and filled with ocean water. "So is that."

"We call those ocean baths. They've been around forever. The sea washes protect the littlies, and they're great for swimming morning laps."

Pausing, they removed their shoes, and then resumed walking along the water's edge where foamy saltwater kissed the white sandy beach. "So what was it like growing up in Beverly Hills?" she asked.

Jake shrugged. "Pretty much like anyplace, except with more Porsches and parents who made movies." He laughed as Elena made a face. "You still had the same teenage angst, pressure to fit in—or not—and study and make grades. It was nice, don't get me wrong, but it isn't necessarily the lavish, dramatic lifestyles the reality shows would have you believe."

"I live there, too. I understand."

"Walls can hide a lot of tragic circumstances, believe me." He shook his head. "Still, my mother is an artist and performer. She thrives on the location and the history, and she has tons of friends there."

She realized she didn't even know where he lived. "Do you live nearby?"

"I have a house in Santa Monica near Montana Avenue." He glanced around. "Can't compare to this beach though."

The Santa Monica beach community in Los Angeles was a well-known haven for those seeking a beach lifestyle in L.A. "I have friends there," Elena said. "We often meet for lunch at one of the cafes on Montana Avenue and then go shopping."

"Where do you like to go?"

Elena named a few places, and soon they were sharing their favorite restaurants and talking about where they liked to go, and what they liked to do on weekends. She realized they had a lot more in common than she'd thought.

Wanting to spend more time with him, she asked if he liked to hike. "The Federation Cliffs have amazing views."

"Lead the way," he said, playfully spinning her around.

They traversed a raised wooden path that hugged the cliffs, stopping to take in the views. Leaning on the wooden rails, she shaded her eyes as she looked out over endless ocean waves.

Elena thought about the surprising turns her life had taken in the last few weeks, and the man who stood beside her. Looking overhead, she saw a few clouds on the horizon, but nothing to be concerned about yet. She was having such a good time that she never wanted this day to end.

Jake seemed different once he opened up. *Maybe that's the armor he has to wear in his line of work*, she thought. He definitely had a softer side that she really liked.

Turning to Jake, she looped her arm through his. "Would you like to see more of Sydney?"

A smile crinkled the corners of his eyes. "If it means seeing more of you."

She caught his hand. "Let's head back. It's easy to get around in this city. Lots of water taxis and ferry boats. We can start at the Royal Botanic Gardens."

Elena loved showing people the gardens, with its giant, two-hundred-year-old watergum and hoop pine trees, aboriginal heritage displays, and lush flowers of every description. She led him into a private tour of the Glass House, thanks to Grams, where they lingered over the vast array of tropical plants, including an incredible of collection of orchids, ferns, bromeliads, lilies, palm trees, and so much more.

The heady aromas were intoxicating. Jake moved closer to her and caught her hand, sending a thrill through her.

In the misty warmth surrounded by the sweet scent of lilies, Jake twirled her into his arms. "Thanks for giving me a second chance."

Elena slid her arms up his shoulders, entwining her hands around his neck. "And me, too." She gazed into his eyes, where she saw the desire growing in her reflected in his. Arching her neck, she brushed her lips along his jaw, teasing him.

Turning into her, Jake caught her lips with his own and enveloped her in his arms.

Warmth gathered in her chest and spread throughout her limbs. Nothing had prepared her for the intensity of his kiss, to which she fully responded, feeling the heat of his passion.

Deepening their kiss, they formed a space all their own in this magical surrounding of nature, and she sank into the soft fullness of his lips. When they finally parted, Elena rested her head against his chest, dizzy with yearning for more.

Jake ran his hands down the length of her back, tracing circles with the palms of his broad hands. "I've been wanting to do that for a long time," he said. "Think they'd find us here if we decided not to leave?"

Elena smiled up at him. "Eventually we'd start growing moss. Wouldn't be a good thing." Far from being sated, the tension she'd felt around him had morphed into a deeper level of longing.

"Guess not," he said, trailing his lips along her neck and pausing to nibble her earlobe. "I'm starving, how about you?"

She giggled. "Are you saying you're hungry for me?" She'd love to lose herself in his arms. Instead, she pressed her fingertips lightly against his chest, putting a little space between them.

"That too. First things first."

"I have an idea. Let's go to the Rocks." One of her best friends from school ran a restaurant and a bed-and-breakfast with her husband there.

"I like the sound of that already."

Laughing, she pulled away and led him outside into the cooler air. Clouds had gathered above. "We still have plenty of time."

They took a water taxi to Circular Quay and walked to the Rocks, meandering through a harbor side market of vendor stalls where local artisans were selling crafts and clothing.

Jake paused by a white-tented stall, admiring a flowing, indigo blue dress paired with a soft pashmina shawl. "This would look incredible on you. Like it?"

"I do." The dress was casual and looked comfortable, and it had sexy cut-outs on the shoulders. Judging by the style, she knew it would fit well. "You have good taste."

"We'll take it," he told the shopkeeper, before hugging Elena to his chest. "It might not be diamonds, but I'd love to see you in this. Oh, I nearly forgot," he said, eyeing high-heeled ankle boots and sandals. "We need to put you in a pair of heels so we can have a proper date."

The shopkeeper overheard his remark and threw a quizzical look their way.

"Inside joke," Elena said, chuckling. She pointed to a pair of deep blue high-heeled booties with lace insets and peep-toes. "What about this pair?"

"Sexy," he said, whistling. "From your nose to your toes." He tapped her nose, and she crinkled it in response. "I love this tiny bling. Blue diamond?"

"But of course," she said, poking him.

"I think it's beautiful."

She grinned. What she didn't say was that in ancient Ayurvedic science, nose piercing was related to women's reproductive systems and believed to make menstrual cycles and childbirth easier. She turned to the shopkeeper. "I'll try those."

She tried on the booties while he helped her zip them

up, looking like he was enjoying the whole process. "Perfect," she said, spinning around. "And I have to get you something authentic, too."

"I have what I want," he said, his voice husky.

The shopkeeper wrapped up their package and Jake paid for it. "Need umbrellas?" she asked.

"I have a hoodie," Elena said.

Jake grinned and kissed her on the cheek. "And I don't mind getting wet."

"Suit yourself," the woman said, shaking her head. "Storm should be coming in soon."

Taking Elena's packages in his hand, Jake peered from the stall. "Now, about that promise of lunch."

"I know just the place," Elena said, shivering slightly. The temperature had dropped and the scent of rain was blowing in over the water. "A friend of mine has a bed-and-breakfast, and her husband is a trained chef. They have a café that's really popular, if we can snag a seat."

"Use your influence," he said as they started off.

They hadn't walked far when sprinkles began to dampen their hair. Elena jerked her hoodie over her hair, while Jake brushed drops from his hair and face.

Seconds later, larger drops began pelting their shoulders. As the sound of rain intensified, people in the market dashed for cover under awnings.

"We should've taken that woman up on the umbrella offer," Jake called out.

"Probably just a quick shower," Elena said, trying to stay positive while trotting for a covered area.

Suddenly, the sky flashed with a bolt of lightning, closely followed by a crack of thunder. A sheet of rain swept over the market area, sending people scrambling for overhangs.

"Run for it!" she cried, stretching her hand out to him through the torrential downpour.

14

HOLDING HANDS, ELENA and Jake sprinted through driving rain to the café. Once under the shelter of the rosy pink awning of Café La Vie, a greenhouse garden oasis in the city, Elena and Jake looked at each other and burst out laughing. They were both drenched. Even her hoodie hadn't offered much protection against the driving rain.

Hurrying inside, the wind slammed the door shut behind them, rattling the botanical prints on the walls. Her friends had bought the old Victorian home and renovated it, turning it into a fashionable café and inn near the harbor.

Elena pushed her hood back and rubbed rain from her eyes. "Hi, Allison." They stood dripping water onto the floor. The lithe blond woman at the front desk looked up in alarm.

"Elena! My God, you're soaked. I'll get some towels for you." Allison bustled to a closet and returned with an armload of towels.

Accepting them, Elena and Jake began to dry off while other guests rushed out past them with umbrellas.

"Everyone is trying to get home before the brunt of the storm hits," Allison said.

"Might be too late for that," Jake said, soaking up the rain they'd tracked in.

"You might be right," Allison said. "The airport is closed, and the ferries and water taxis are staying put."

Elena pushed her fingers through her damp hair. "Then we're not going anywhere for a while. Maybe it will let up while we have lunch." However, she realized it wasn't likely. She should have listened to her mother's warning this morning. "Is Zach in the kitchen?"

"He is. We've already sent the kitchen staff home." Allison reached for menus. "We're usually fully reserved for lunch, but not today." She showed them to a table.

A little drier but still shivering, Elena sat down.

"Cold?" Jake pulled his chair next to hers, put his arm around her, and rubbed her arm. She snuggled into the curve of his warm body.

"What sounds good to you?" Jake held a menu, and they read it together. "Duck confit salad, chilled seafood tower, pumpkin bisque…"

"Hmm, yes, yes, and yes." Everything sounded delicious, and Zach was an excellent chef.

"I forgot I'm with a lady who likes to eat."

Jake ordered, and Allison brought out a bottle of red wine and bread for the table, followed by the bisque. "This should warm you up," she said.

The last of the lunch crowd had left, so Elena asked Allison to join them. "Share a glass of wine with us?"

Elena and Allison caught up while Zach brought the rest of their lunch to the table. As they ate, the lightning and thunder intensified.

"Wonder when this will let up?" Elena dipped a piece of Zach's crusty homemade bread into olive oil. She was hungrier than she'd thought.

Zach drew a hand over his chin. "This is one of the worst storms we've had in years. It's supposed to get a lot worse."

With the city shutting down, Elena was worried. "How can we get back to Bondi Beach?"

"I don't think you can," Allison said. "I heard the streets are flooding, so no one is going anywhere. We've just had a room cancellation. You're welcome to stay here tonight."

Overhead, the glass panels of the greenhouse roof began to leak, dripping onto their table.

Zach stood up. "I was afraid of that."

"I've got towels and buckets," Allison said, starting to rise.

"I'll give him a hand," Jake said, getting up to help him. The two men began to place buckets in strategic spots.

Allison shot Elena a look of concern. "This could flood, so we'd better move into the main house. It's built higher up." She led Elena through a doorway and up steps into the old Victorian home.

"You've done even more than the last time I saw it,"

Elena said, glancing around the high-ceilinged salon. The walls were painted a muted shade of rose, and fresh flowers graced the entryway. Any other time, she'd love to stay here for a relaxing weekend, but she was worried about the storm.

"It's been a long process. We renovated the guestrooms, too." A smile lit Allison's face. "Jake seems awfully nice, and I'm glad he's helping Zach. How long have you been dating?"

"Not long." Certainly not long enough to be checking into an inn together. She trembled from the chill and damp clothes. "Do you have another room, too?"

"We're full except for this cancellation." Allison reached behind the reception desk for a key. "This is one of my favorite rooms. Top of the stairs to the left."

Elena studied the old skeleton key in her hand. They were both adults. They could figure something out.

Frowning, Allison touched her hand. "There's a couch if you're worried about him. Or you could stay with us in our suite. It's a little small, though. For now, we're renting out the larger rooms."

Elena shook her head. "No, it's fine." It wasn't that she didn't trust him—it was her own feelings she didn't trust.

"Problem?" Zach came in, followed by Jake. They must have been outside, because both men were soaked.

"We're just getting settled," Allison said. "You'll find robes there, and I can dry your clothes if you'd like."

Jake dangled the plastic shopping bag they'd left at the table. "Fortunately, you've got dry clothes." Taking care not to get her any wetter than she already was, he kissed Elena's cheek. "Come on, let's get you out of those wet clothes."

Elena couldn't help herself. She burst out laughing and tapped his chest. "You have no idea how that sounds." *Not that it's a bad idea…*

"Don't I?" He grinned and kissed her while Allison and Zach laughed.

"Come join us later for a glass of wine," Zach said. "Since no one can go out, I'm making supper for everyone. You'll find candles and torches in the room in case we lose power." When Jake looked confused, he grinned. "That's 'flashlights' for you Yanks."

When they reached the door to the room, Jake opened it and offered her his hand. Slipping her cold, quivering hand in his, Elena caught her breath as she stepped inside.

"Allison outdid herself," she said, taking in their surroundings. Decorated in shades of blush pink and white, the room was the epitome of Victorian luxury. Fresh lilies and roses adorned the entry table.

Through rain-streaked windows, Elena could see the Sydney Harbour Bridge stretching into dense, blackened clouds. A seating arrangement with mauve pillows anchored a brick fireplace where a low gas flame flickered. Jazz music filtered through the room. *So soothing, so romantic.* The atmosphere seeped into her like a salve, easing the stress she'd been under.

Coming up behind her, Jake enveloped her in his arms

and nuzzled her neck. "How do you do it? You're spectacular, even all wet. But just because we're here, doesn't mean I expect anything of you."

Elena turned and flung her arms around him. As her lips found the warmth of his, her shivering lessened.

Jake pulled away. "Elena, I'm serious. I respect you and if you don't—"

"I'm serious, too. You're sleeping on the couch." Laughing nervously, she led him to the small loveseat in front of the crackling fireplace. With his tall frame, she realized it was a ridiculous proposition.

"You've got to be kidding." Jake put his hands on his hips. "But okay. The floor's good, too. You get the bed." Stepping in front of the fireplace, he peeled off his soggy sweatshirt. "Robes in the closet, right?"

Watching, Elena could only nod. *What a physique... Broad chest, hard body, narrow hips.*

"You should change. I'll bring one for you, too."

After he left the room, she whirled around and bit down on her finger to keep from crying out. How was she ever going to sleep with him in the next room? Recalling the passion of his kiss earlier today, she knew it would be nearly impossible.

Having changed into a dry robe, Jake sauntered back in and handed her one. "Are you okay? You should really get out of those wet things. You're still trembling." He stepped toward her and rubbed her arms.

"I will in a minute." But first, unable to resist the temptation, she moved the terry cloth to one side and slid her fingers over the upper part of his chest that peeked out. Exploring, she closed her eyes, imagining what it would be like. She drew her hand back, but he caught it and kissed her fingertips. Her resolve was melting. Was it him, or a desire to be free from the strain of all she'd been through the past week, even for a few hours?

Jake tipped her chin up and brought his lips tentatively to hers.

Responding, she felt herself craving his touch, needing him to soothe her frayed nerves. She slid her hand over his chest again.

With a moan, he enfolded her in his arms, peppering her damp face with kisses.

Outside, the storm was intensifying, matching the blood pumping through her veins. While her emotions warred, the scale tipped as her need for him outweighed her reticence.

"Help me get changed?" She led him into the bedroom and pulled him onto the plush duvet-covered bed.

With a deliberate motion, he smoothed her damp hair from her forehead, and then drew his hands alongside her cheeks, cradling her face between his hands. He stared at her for a long moment with an expression she could only describe as one of adoration. Catching her breath, she drew her lower lip between her teeth.

"Just wait," he murmured, his voice deepening. "I want

to remember you like this, right now, forever."

Reaching up, she ran a hand through his wet hair. His eyes were intently focused on her, and the emotion in his face was nearly overwhelming. *This feels so real, so right.* Wordlessly, she met the intensity of his gaze, no longer caring about anything but living in the moment.

"Let's take our time." He lowered himself onto her, exploring her lips, her neck, and her shoulders.

She lifted herself up to shed her wet clothes. Feeling his bare skin pressed against hers was the most incredible sensation she'd ever felt. Sighing with pleasure, she ran her hands down the length of his back and hips.

Easing her under the duvet onto a silky cotton sheet, he paused for a moment, raising his dark brows. "Are you sure this is okay?"

She nodded her assent, needing to feel cared for, needing his caress. He continued his exploration of her shivering body—only now she quivered with anticipation.

Dragging his lips across her stomach, he moved slowly, deliberately, rhythmically.

Together they held each other, getting to know each other in the most intimate way. He touched her in ways she'd never dreamed—physically and emotionally. Even the way he whispered her name was musical.

Holding him to her chest, she ran her fingers along his broad back as if to memorize every sinew and muscle. He was the most perfect specimen of a man she could have ever designed.

Lost in each other, they were oblivious to the relentless rain that blotted out the daylight, ushering in an early evening. Hours later, they lay tangled in each other's limbs, fully sated and yet still yearning for more.

Afterward, he got up to run a bath. When Elena followed him into the bathroom, she sat next to him, wrapped in her robe. Fluffy bisque and rose towels were piled everywhere, and a glass enclosure featured a rain-shower head suspended from the ceiling. Music was piped in, and orange citrus potpourri scented the air. She breathed out, feeling more relaxed than she had in a long, long time.

"This is exactly what I needed," she said, twirling her fingers in the water. The wide oblong bath was large enough for the two of them.

She poured foaming bath oil into the running water he'd adjusted to just the right temperature, releasing the scent of sweet verbena. Crystal bowls of nuts, dried apricots, and chocolates lined the tub, along with an ice bucket with a bottle of chilled champagne standing ready. Allison had thought of everything for her guests.

"Get in, I'll be there in a moment." Jake stopped to light the candles that surrounded the tub before turning out the lights.

Elena eased her spent body into the swirling warm water amid mounds of bubbles billowing from gently throbbing jets. Laughing, she scooped up a handful of bubbles and blew them through the air to float down like tiny snowflakes.

Jake opened the champagne and poured two flutes. Sliding in beside her, he handed her a glass. "To you," he said, smiling at her with the most wondrous expression. "And to your grandparents, who kept throwing us together until we stuck."

While they sipped their champagne, they chatted about the adventure they'd had today, laughing at their experiences. Jake fed her cashews, almonds, and pistachios, and she reciprocated with dark chocolate bon-bons dusted with cocoa powder that melted in their mouths.

"You know we're having dessert first," she said, licking chocolate from her fingers.

"Yes, we did." He kissed the tip of her nose. "Life is short, you can never have too much dessert."

When the water grew cool, they stepped from the bath and toweled each other off, snuggling back into the terry cloth robes before lounging in front of the fireplace.

Outside, rain continued to pelt the windows, while strong winds bowed palm trees and rattled the inn's wood frame structure. Suddenly, a loud hammering noise against the house erupted.

"What the heck?" Jake stood and strode to the window. "Hail, and it's big." He pulled the shades and jerked the draperies across all the windows.

After returning to her and wrapping his arms around her, he said, "Elena, I have to be honest with you. When I stepped off the plane in Sydney, this was the farthest thing from my mind, but it's the most perfect thing that's ever happened to me. Thank you for believing in me, and seeing past my thorny exterior and lousy manners."

His words touched her heart. "We both let our guard down, and I'm really glad we did." She hoped it would last once they returned to the reality of L.A. She stroked his face and leaned in to kiss him, and as their lips met, the lights snapped off.

"That was one powerful kiss," he said. By firelight, they lit a trio of candles on the coffee table.

A knocking sounded at the door. "Are you okay in there?" It was Zach. "Sorry, we just lost electricity. Probably won't come back on any time soon. If you'd like to come downstairs, I've made a pot of bouillabaisse with salad and flatbread. And some good wine."

Jake looked to Elena, who nodded. "We'd like that. We'll see you downstairs."

After Zach left, they dressed. Jake had draped his clothes on top of the old radiator so they were dry, while Elena put on her new indigo blue dress and swirled around.

"That color lights up your eyes," he said, drawing his arms around her. As Elena arched her neck, he kissed her on her shoulders and worked his way up her neck.

Jake paused, lightly touching the discreet tattoo she had on her neck just behind her ear. "I've been meaning to ask you what kind of flower this is."

"It's a lotus blossom."

"Beautiful. Did you know those are revered in the east?"

She tapped his nose. "Of course I do. The lotus is a symbol of divinity and enlightenment in India. Have you ever been there?"

He nodded, grinning. "Couple of years ago with my mom. We went to a Bollywood-Meets-Hollywood festival. We had a great time there." A smiled danced on his lips. "Does India hold special significance for you?"

Elena caught her lip between her teeth. It had tremendous significance, and they'd taken a huge step today, but she wasn't sure she was ready to bare this deepest part of her soul to him yet.

Instead, she simply said, "It does."

15

LIGHTNING ILLUMINATED THE old Victorian stairway as Elena and Jake made their way downstairs. A flash rendered the salon in stark relief and she gripped the bannister.

A crack of thunder quickly followed, shaking the house.

The storm was getting worse, and as much as Elena loved being alone with Jake, she felt better that they were all together.

"Wow," Jake said. "That was pretty impressive."

"Hurry down," Allison called out, pouring red wine into a pair of goblets. Candle flickered around the room, and a fire blazed in the corner, while music from a portable stereo made the atmosphere less scary and more festive. Looking apprehensive, another couple clung to each other on a sofa. Zach was busy spooning bouillabaisse into large soup bowls. "Figured we might as well make it a party."

"That's what I love about Australia," Elena said. "No matter how dark things are, it's always time for a party."

"What else can we do?" Zach said. "We've already got the sandbags on the perimeter. If the water rises, we'll take the party up to our room. Or yours—your choice, mate," he added with a hearty laugh. "Have a seat."

Elena shot a look at Jake to make sure he was okay with the Aussie sense of humor, but he was fine. She slid her arm around him, and he planted a kiss on her forehead. This was all she'd ever wanted in a relationship. Someone she felt comfortable with, who was also smart, exciting, fun, and great with her family—the whole package. *And a great kisser,* she added to the list. *He's the whole package, for sure.*

Zach placed steaming bowls of seafood in a spiced broth on the low coffee table before them. The scent of toasted garlic flatbread made Elena realize how hungry she was again. Zach still wore his white chef's jacket, and his blond hair that had been longer when they were younger was now cropped short. He touched his wine glass to theirs. "Welcome to the land of Aus," he said, his shortened pronunciation sounding like *oz.*

Another flash of hail littered the side of the house, and everyone instinctively ducked. "No worries," Zach said. "She's stood for a century. She probably won't succumb tonight."

Allison folded her legs under her on the sofa. "So, Elena, you didn't tell me you were dating anyone, let alone someone as fabulous-looking as Jake. We're not besties anymore?"

"Some things I like to keep to myself," Elena said,

hugging Jake. She heard a little slur in Allison's voice, but then, she was also feeling pretty relaxed from the champagne…*and dessert*, she thought to herself with a smile.

Jake grinned, glancing between Allison and Elena.

"Well done, you," Allison said. Turning to Jake, she added, "If you're wondering why we're all a bit bonkers, we went to school together. The old Bondi gang, that's us." She raised her wine glass, chuckling.

Waves of thunder rolled across the city outside as if for emphasis.

"Allison and I are like sisters," Elena said. "We were inseparable for years."

"We're awful proud of this one for getting out and going after what she wants," Zach said. "We had an Academy Awards party so all of us could ogle Penelope Plessen and Elena's diamonds on the big screen."

Allison topped off the other couple's glasses. Bringing them into the conversation, she said, "Elena designed the jewelry Penelope wore that night. Did you hear about the robbery?"

Noticing Elena's downcast eyes, Allison pressed her hand against her mouth. "Oh, I'm sorry, Elena. You probably don't want to talk about that."

Elena lifted her shoulder and let it fall. "It's okay. It happened."

Jake took her hand and squeezed it. "I'm helping her find the perps," he said with a straight face. Then he winked at her.

He sounded so much like a tough character out of *Law and Order*, Elena would've laughed out loud if her loss hadn't been so painful.

"Impressive," Allison said. "Well, we always knew Elena was destined for greatness. She's descended from an Indian princess, after all." As soon as the words slipped out, Allison clamped her hand over her mouth.

"Allison!" Elena glared at her.

"I'm sorry," she said, wincing. "I know I promised." She made a zipping motion across her mouth with her fingers.

Horrified that her friend had uttered a secret she'd told her in strictest confidence years ago, Elena managed a feeble laugh. "We made up a lot of stories back then."

Jake chuckled and changed the subject, asking Zach about where he'd learned to cook.

Elena let out a little breath, relieved that he hadn't pursued Allison's comment. She hoped that would be the end of it.

In time, the rain lessened, and Elena and Jake said goodnight to everyone and returned to their suite. Elena tried to act as though nothing had happened, but she could tell that Jake sensed a change in her.

That night, Jake slept with his arms around her, while she curled her body into the curve of his long frame. Whatever she was, wherever she had come from, mattered little to her in that moment. She'd discovered a precious connection with Jake. Whatever the past, her future lay ahead. It was unwritten, yet she wondered if she must reveal the truth the women in her family had shielded for generations in order to pen the future she desired.

Sabeena's secret.

She didn't want to keep anything from Jake. But was it time? Was it safe?

This weight she carried—it wasn't her secret to share. Or was it? Had the edges of these rocks that had tumbled through time to her not been worn smooth by the labor of her ancestors?

Elena lay awake thinking. This secret she carried had guided her life in a way none of her friends could imagine. She was a modern woman. She believed that she alone created her own destiny. Lana and Honey had taught her that. Yet, was she far enough removed from the bondage of the past that the tentacles of history could not reach her?

Or, more important, was her grandmother?

By the next morning, the skies had cleared and rays of sunshine bled through the edges of the draperies Jake had drawn against the icy hail.

Elena stretched luxuriantly, thinking about the connection she'd found with Jake between the sheets the night before. Smiling to herself, she pulled the covers to her nose, reliving the delights they'd discovered between them.

"Hey bright eyes, good morning." Jake stepped from the

bathroom, his hair damp and a towel tucked around his hips.

"Hmm, good morning. So last night wasn't a dream?"

He crossed to the bed and raised her to him, enclosing her within his muscular arms. "It was the best dream I've ever had. And I hope it never ends. Think we can order another storm today?"

"I think I feel one gathering on the horizon right now." She teased his lips with her tongue until he could no longer resist her, and once again, she let herself be carried away with their passion, thinking of nothing else but the desire that united them.

Finally, spent once again, Elena flung herself against a mound of pillows, happiness washing over her like the waves at Bondi Beach.

With that thought, she opened her eyes. "Although I wish we could hide in this cocoon forever, I need to go home and check on my dad." She'd texted them yesterday to let them know they were safe during the storm.

"I understand." Jake rolled next to her. "Let's have lunch before we leave."

"Is it already that time?"

"You slept until noon, princess."

Elena shot him a look, but by his innocent expression, it didn't seem he'd meant to instill any special meaning into his choice of words.

After enjoying a thorough, luxurious drenching under the ceiling-mounted rain-shower, Elena toweled off and put on the new indigo dress they'd bought yesterday. Peering into the mirror, she wondered if the emotional shifts she felt inside were somehow visible on the outside.

She was still Elena Eaton, and yet, she'd become even more so. Confident, loved, and loving. She felt a new dimension of her life opening before her. One she'd hoped for, but had almost given up imagining might be possible.

Jake appeared behind her. Resting his hands on her shoulders, he tenderly kissed her neck. "You're the most fascinating woman I've ever known. And ever hope to."

She ran a hand over his and turned into his arms. What mere words could express the feeling in her heart? Grazing his lips with hers, she heard his stomach rumble again.

"Shh," he whispered, feigning embarrassment.

Smiling into his lips, she said, "Who's hungry?"

Jake took her by the hand and they went downstairs.

"Good afternoon," Allison said, her eyes twinkling.

"Room for two in the café?" Jake asked.

"Absolutely. I saved a table for you," Allison said, showing them the way.

Every table was filled with people enjoying themselves in the sunshine that filtered through glass panels overhead. Inside, the scents of saffron, garlic, and oregano tantalized, while outside, lush foliage, the soaring Sydney Harbour Bridge, and cloudless blue skies filled the view.

Jake stopped by the kitchen to say hello to Zach, who was leading a small team in lunch preparations, and they began to chat about the menu.

Before Elena sat down, Allison leaned in and whispered, "I was an idiot last night for saying…you know." Her fair complexion reddened with embarrassment.

"It's okay."

"It was the wine talking." She tucked a blond strand behind her ear, casting her eyes down in embarrassment. "I need to cut back, but I swear I've never mentioned a word to another soul, especially my lousy brother, Shane. I'm just so proud of all you've done."

"I believe you, and it's all right." Elena clasped Allison's hand, forgiving her friend. She'd almost forgotten that in a fit of teenage rebellion against her parents, she'd confided in Allison. All these years, Allison had never betrayed her secret. One slip up she could forgive. "I haven't shared that with Jake yet, so let me be the one, okay?"

"I won't say another word. Ever. To anyone."

Elena hoped Jake had forgotten about Allison's comment. It wasn't even a relevant part of her story. She was simply Elena of Bondi Beach.

"Tell your family hello for me," Allison said. "Running this place, we don't get to the beach much anymore." With excitement etched on her face, she leaned in. "And we want to start trying for a baby."

"That's wonderful," Elena said, pleased for her.

"So you see, I do plan to cut out all alcohol." Allison smiled broadly.

"I wish you the best. You'll make a great mother." She hugged her friend before Allison excused herself to see to another guest.

"Lunch will be here shortly." Jake eased into a chair beside her.

Elena crossed her arms in mock outrage. "One night of passion and you think you can just take over my life and start ordering my food for me?"

Grinning, he replied, "I know what you like. Besides, it was Zach's idea,' he added, jerking his thumb toward the kitchen.

"Don't push it off on him." Smiling, she reached for his hand. "Can't wait. I love surprises."

Soon Zach begin to send out a variety of small dishes, from butternut squash soup to tangy mussels and a crunchy seaweed salad, to a crab and fruit salad loaded with kiwi, mango, and berries. Just when she thought she could eat no more, a silky dark chocolate mousse with raspberries and passion fruit sauce appeared.

"I feel thoroughly indulged," she said as she scooped a bite.

"By me or Zach?"

Elena cupped her hand in her chin. "I'll have to think about that. Can you cook?"

Entwining his fingers in hers, he said, "You just wait. You have no idea."

"Oh really?" she asked, baiting him.

"You know those cooking classes for men that Lance has been offering at Bow-Tie?"

She laughed. "I heard about them." The classes were good publicity for the restaurant, and Lance and Johnny had involved some local celebrities, then shared profits with the Big Brothers charity group. She had a similar idea for something that would benefit the women's charity she volunteered with.

"Stefan and I went. We actually learned a lot."

"Penelope did mention something." Elena furrowed her brow. "By the way, do you know if Johnny has been cleared of suspicion in the robbery?"

"He has, and I'm glad." Jake traced a lazy circle on her hand.

"What a relief." She'd been concerned for Johnny and Scarlett.

Giving her the last bite of the chocolate mousse, he said, "I like having friends over to the house to cook and watch a game, or hang out by the pool. Maybe we could invite Stefan and Penelope, along with Lance and Johnny. "

"And Verena and Scarlett. Surely if Johnny was investigated, you know he's dating my friend Scarlett."

"The attorney." Jake smiled. "Her name came up several times, and she sounds quite accomplished. I hope to meet her soon."

Elena liked that he was planning for when they returned and including her friends. From her volunteer work at the shelter, she knew that when men wanted to separate women from their friends or family, it was a red flag for the potential of mental or physical abuse.

However, the thought of returning to California also jolted her back to reality. Orders from her website had been piling up—fortunately. Her father was greatly improved, and eventually she'd only be in the way of her parents. They'd already promised to take time off in the winter to come for a visit, and the doctor thought Gabe would be well enough to travel in a few weeks as long as he promised not to lift suitcases.

She'd also have to face the consequences of the robbery—whatever they might be. It was more important than ever that she talk to Grams for advice.

Her future with Jake might rest on it.

16

WHEN HIS ALARM blared before dawn, Jake was still in the throes of a marvelous dream of Elena that he never wanted to end. He reached out to stroke her back.

All he met with was an empty spot on his hotel bed. Realizing she wasn't there, he punched the pillow beside him and slapped the alarm.

The day of the storm, they'd had such an extraordinary time. Though he hadn't been expecting her to fall into bed with him, he'd been thrilled. Their connection had been absolutely sensational. Never before had he experienced that level of physical or emotional intimacy.

Stefan had said something to him about his relationship with Penelope that Jake recalled now. *You might not know when it's wrong, but you sure know when it's right.*

Jake stretched in bed as he thought of this. That's exactly how he felt now. In retrospect, he and Jenny had just been going through the motions, each them being pleasant enough, but the magic had been missing.

He'd sure found the magic with Elena.

Locking his hands under his head, he stared out at the pre-dawn harbor view from the window of the high-rise hotel where he was staying. Just thinking about her brought a smile to his face.

Scrubbing his hands through his hair, he swung his legs over the edge of the bed, remembering that he'd promised her grandfather that he'd go fishing with him today. A thought crept into his mind.

Jake had yet to accomplish what he came here for, which was to answer the questions the insurance company had about the veracity of the value of Elena's diamonds. Just a few days ago he'd been convinced she was guilty of something because of the way she'd shot out of the country.

That was before he'd known her father had suffered a cardiac arrest. Jake felt guilty about that now. When he'd tracked her to her parents' home, he'd run a cross check to obtain their phone number and called. Thinking he was a friend from America, Honey had told him she'd gone to the opera. Meeting Elena there had been no accident, and her grandfather had played right into his hand.

Jake adjusted the shower and stepped in, letting the cool water sluice over his warm body. Placing his hands against the cool tiles, he began to laugh at himself. Maybe he'd let himself get taken in by her grandparents. They were such decent people. As were Honey and Gabe. He even liked her friends, Allison and Zach. *What a chef he is*, he thought, looking forward to a friendship with the couple. He truly liked Elena's friends.

Now he felt sure Elena was telling the truth about the diamonds. His dilemma was how to support the value for her. If only she'd be more forthright with him. He was convinced she was hiding something—they all were—but what could it be?

Most of stones had come from India, of that much he was fairly certain. Elena and Lana had admitted that. And then Allison had made a silly comment that now didn't seem so frivolous.

Or was he simply reading more into it?

Suddenly he remembered one of his buddies took his little daughter to some sort of an Indian Princess group for adventure outings. He chuckled to himself. Gabe was a good guy, and he could just imagine the two of them together when Elena was a little girl. They probably went camping with other dads and daughters.

Still pondering the issue of the diamonds and their value, he shook water from his hair and stepped from the shower to get ready. On the other hand, if one of Elena's ancestors had been a jewel thief, why would she have paraded stolen gems at the Academy Awards? She was smarter than that.

Not that thieves were usually known for their intelligence. Or was the case so old that it had grown cold?

All he had to prove was that the diamonds were real and the value could be verified.

Pulling on a pair of jeans and a sweatshirt, he decided to appeal again to Elena's grandfather. Maybe he'd share the story privately.

Jake had nothing but admiration for Aaron, who had an old fishing vessel he took Jake out on to share his best fishing spots. Waves lapped the edges, gently rocking the boat as dawn streaked the sky with fiery orange and yellow. Birds twittered in trees around them and the scent of marine kelp filled his nostrils.

Jake was the one trying to obtain more details, however, it hadn't taken Elena's grandfather long to launch into his explorations once they had dropped lines into the water. Aaron pulled a cap over his silver hair and sat down beside him, the weathered deck creaking under his step. "We like you Jake, like you a lot. Your family from Los Angeles?"

"Yes, sir. Dad moved there as a little boy. Started an insurance company that grew to be one of the largest on the west coast."

"So you probably had the benefit of a good education."

"Yes, sir."

"Explains your fine manners—not that you need an education for that. No, indeed. That's life education." Feeling a light tug on his line, he reeled in a little, then a little more. Nothing. He cast again. "How about your mother?"

Here we go, Jake thought. "My mother is Barbara Charles."

"You don't say?"

Aaron's surprise was genuine, so Jake surmised that Elena hadn't mentioned it. He liked that. Usually that was one of the first things his dates told their friends and family.

"She's one of my favorite actresses. Beautiful woman, if you don't mind my saying. Doesn't do a bad Australian accent, either. Not perfect, but not bad."

Jake opened his mouth to protest, and then shut it. He couldn't argue that point with an Australian. Now he felt like an idiot for accusing Elena of faking her accent when he'd first met her.

"So what brings you to Sydney? Followed Elena, did you? She's a lovely young woman."

"I'm a lucky guy. She means a lot to me." Jake checked his line, stalling for a moment to choose his next words with care. "I followed Elena here, but not for the reason you think."

"Oh?"

"Penelope Plessen, the model who wore her necklace at the Academy Awards, filed an insurance claim for the loss. That will help Elena recover her loss because Penelope assumed financial responsibility."

"Lana told me you were helping Elena in some way. Didn't she have insurance?"

"It ceased when the jewelry left her possession. Only the larger jewelers have the financial capacity to carry broad insurance that would have covered such loaning." Jake pitched forward in his chair. "It's a fairly complicated undertaking to loan millions of dollars of jewelry for stars to wear to public events. But the advertising value is well worth the risk."

Taking in Jake's words, Aaron nodded. "Which is why Elena took that risk. If Penelope is covered, then why are you involved?"

"It's pretty standard on large losses."

"I see. Don't the police track the thieves?"

"They do, along with the FBI. If I come across information that can help them I share it, but in this case, I was hired for other reasons."

"What would those be?"

"To verify value. Make sure the jewelry is properly valued so Elena can be compensated for her loss. Old receipts, anything, would help."

Aaron threw a warning glance his way. "Can't help you there, son."

Jake drew his chair closer. "Whatever you tell me I'll keep in confidence. I don't have to share details with the authorities."

Aaron shook his head.

"Why wouldn't you want Elena to recover her loss?"

"Look out there," Aaron said, waving toward the skyline of Sydney behind them. "We've built a good life here. Lots of friends. Good health. Enjoying the years we have left."

"What does that have to do with Elena?"

Placing his hands on his knees, he slowly turned to Jake. "Some things are more important than money, son."

"But why—"

"It's not my story to tell." Aaron stood, and shoved his hands into his pockets.

"Whose is it?"

"My wife's. And I will protect her right not to share it until my last breath. So will Elena." He turned to look at the dawning sky. "You're a good lad, but you'll find no answers here."

"I understand, sir," Jake said. "I would do the same for Elena. Although I hate to see her lose a fortune. I'd like to help." He also felt a strong need to know the truth.

Frustrated, Jake knew if he couldn't establish value, there was no sense pursuing this matter any longer for the insurance company.

Aaron ran a finger along the boat's weathered wood. "There was never a financial cost associated with the diamonds, so in a way, there's no loss. See if you can look at it that way. That's all I'm going to say."

Feeling defeated, Jake shook his head. There was no point arguing. The best he could do for Elena would be to get the cost of her other materials, such as the expensive platinum she used.

Yet, he still wrestled with his need to know the truth about the woman he'd fallen in love with. Wasn't that only fair?

Aaron crossed the deck to Jake and rested a hand on his shoulder. "Elena's a smart, talented young woman. We all have confidence in her."

17

"JAKE CAN STAY with us in Rushcutters Bay," Lana said. "There's no need for him to stay in a hotel."

"His company is covering it." Holding a straw basket over her arm, Elena strolled beside her grandmother at the Bondi Beach outdoor market.

The sky was brilliant today, and the market was teeming with people who'd spent yesterday cleaning up after the storm. When she'd returned home with Jake, her mother and father had insisted that he stay for a family dinner. Grams and Gramps had joined them, and Jake had spent a long time talking to Aaron and her dad.

"That's not the point," Lana said, selecting tomatoes from a vendor's display. "We'd enjoy having him around. He and Aaron have really hit it off."

"Nice of Gramps to take him fishing today." Elena ignored her question by tasting strawberries a vendor offered before she choose some. Jake had invited her to his hotel after he returned, and she could hardly wait to see him again.

"I hope it didn't interfere with his work here." Her grandmother waved at a group of ladies she knew as they passed. With a sparkle in her eye, she said, "You and Jake seem to have buried your differences, whatever they were."

"We had a talk." Elena felt her cheeks flush.

"Is that what they call it now?" She pointed out a couple of passion fruits to the stall vendor. "I'll take those two. They look ripe, yes?" She slid a glance toward Elena.

The comparison wasn't lost on her. Grams had always been forthright about her observations. Yet she was intensely private about other matters.

"About his work, Grams. There's something I need to talk to you about."

Lana paid for the fruit and put it into Elena's basket. "We've had this discussion. If what had happened had been today, and not a hundred years ago, it would have been different. You know that. But we are a product of our time. We don't get to choose when we're born. *That* matters." She held a firm expression, her lips pressed together. "Especially for women."

As she followed her grandmother around, Elena wondered what she would have done then. And what she should do now.

Later that afternoon, Elena arrived at the high-rise hotel

where Jake was staying. She'd bought another new casual dress at the market with her grandmother, and borrowed one of her mother's lightweight apricot sweaters to throw over her shoulders when it got cooler.

She liked adding accessories, so she chose coral earrings and bracelets that she'd made for her mother years ago from Honey's collection, and dabbed on a bit of her mum's ambery perfume from a local brand she liked. *Bohemia.* That was fitting, she thought with a smile.

When Jake opened the door, he swept her into his arms. Lifting her from her feet, he twirled her around. "I've been dying to see you," he said, kissing her. "And you smell delicious."

Laughing, Elena ruffled his hair, and then smoothed it back. As she did, her gaze rested on his open suitcase. It was neatly packed, and his toiletries were on top. "Going somewhere?"

"Ah, yeah, about that..."

"Maybe there's room again at Allison and Zach's place." Playfully, she pursed her lips.

"No..."

Remembering what Grams had said, she blurted out, "Please don't go to Rushcutters Bay with my grandparents."

He shook his head. "My work is finished here, Elena, and I'm needed at the office. I'm catching a flight back tonight."

"Why?" She felt the excitement of seeing him drain from

her.

"You know why I came here. While I believe you now, there's nothing more I can do to help you. Whatever your family is hiding will remain that way."

Feeling like he was abandoning her, Elena folded her arms and turned away, staring out the wide glass windows overlooking the Sydney Harbour Bridge. She was hurt that he was leaving simply because he couldn't get the information he wanted from them. "Is that the only reason you were staying?"

"Elena, it's not too late to tell me what's going on."

He didn't answer her question. She swung back to him. "It's not what you think it is."

Jake put his hands on his hips. "Look, I don't care if someone in your family stole the diamonds, found them in an alley, or won them in a game of strip poker. All I was trying to do was make sure you were fairly compensated for your loss."

She stared at him, hardly believing what she was hearing. Letting his words sink in, she asked the question she was afraid of. "And what happened here with us…was it only about finding out the truth?" Bristling, she forged on, unable to stop. "Or maybe that's a technique you use in your investigations with women. And now that you can't get what you want, you're on the next flight out."

"You can't believe any of that." Jake stood in front of her, his lips pressed firmly together.

"I don't *want* to believe that, but there's the evidence." Her anger rising, she pointed to his suitcase. "So what's that really about?"

"Your Gramps set me straight. The loss isn't what's important here."

Elena paced the length of the window. "Last I heard, Gramps really liked you. I don't know what you said on that fishing boat today to change that."

"Nothing happened."

"Don't patronize me." Elena crossed her arms. She hated that more than anything.

"I don't mean to." Jake spread out his hands. "I'm not part of this family, so whatever secret your grandmother is hiding is none of my business. You need to spend time with your father, and when you return—"

"Why should I ever return?" she asked, willing him to give her a reason. Had the declarations he'd made to her during their night of passion meant nothing?

Drawing his dark eyebrows together, he seemed confused. "Your shop, your friends. You can recover from this loss. I'll get you something for the materials you used. Platinum is expensive."

"This is not about platinum, or friends, or my shop. This is about family, and where you stand with me, whether you know my family's entire story or not."

Jake threw his hands in the air. "I don't know what you want from me."

"Only one thing." How could he not see how much pain this was causing her?

"I don't how to help you."

"I never asked for your help." Elena bit her lip. "Good manners means accepting people as they are, and not browbeating them for the truth."

Jake held up a finger. "I did *not* do that."

"Didn't you? Every chance you got with my grandparents. And it's not my story to tell." Hurt and anger surged through her. "Not yet, anyway."

Leaving Jake to figure it out on his own, she strode across the room, flung open the door, and marched out.

As the elevator doors closed, this time, she noticed, he didn't come after her. Clutching her arms around her, she fought the tears that filled her eyes.

18

ELENA SAT IN front of her mother's computer in the cottage listlessly checking emails that had come in for orders from her website. She was thankful to see them, though her excitement was dimmed due to Jake's sudden departure,

It was another beautiful morning in Sydney, sunny and bright, with kookaburra birds laughing at her folly just outside the window.

She'd sank almost everything she owned into the jewelry that Penelope had worn, and now the gamble was beginning to pay off as photos were published and her website and shop address were included in fashion editors' top picks. Only she was no longer there to take advantage of it.

Tapping replies—certain pieces were now backordered—she thought, *not that I can't work from anywhere in the world.* She could get supplies here, set up shop, and return to doing the work she missed.

Close my place in L.A.

And never see Jake again.

Since Jake left, she'd vowed to do just as he'd suggested, which was to spend time with her father and her family—the people she could be sure loved her just as she was.

"Hey, little fairy-wren."

Elena looked up. Her father was walking pretty well now. "How're you feeling, Dad?"

"Lot better than you look."

She made a face.

"You've been in front of that computer for too many hours these past few days." He rapped his knuckles on the table beside her. "Go for a walk with me?"

"Sure." She pushed away from the computer and padded to her old room to get her sand shoes. The physical therapists recommended a short walk every day for him now.

They stepped outside and slowly made their way toward the beach, where she'd walked with Jake the morning of the storm she'd never forget.

Gabe slid a look in her direction. "Sure wish I didn't feel like I was all alone out here."

Elena's mouth fell open. "I'm here, Dad."

"Your mind is a thousand kilometers away. Or more like twelve thousand. I believe that's how far L.A. is, right?"

She raised a shoulder and let it drop. "I want to be here with you."

"I'm your dad. I can tell when you're restless." He draped his arm around her as they walked along the water's edge.

"Hi, Mr. Gabe," a young surfing boy called out.

"Looking good there," a lifeguard yelled. "How's Honey?"

"Tired of me being under foot." Her father waved to them and a few others who lined the shore.

"Get back to work, you lazy arse," called another friend.

Gabe laughed off his comment.

Elena watched her father acknowledging others on the beach. This was his world, where he and her mother belonged. Where they had chosen to be. Not in a high-rise condo in Sydney, or a suburb near Melbourne. Or anywhere in the world, for that matter. Right here because they loved it.

Where was her place?

She raised her face to the cool ocean mist, letting it blow through her heated mind.

Her dad slowed, filling his lungs with sea air. "Hear much from Jake?"

"Nope." She could almost hear the cogs turning in her dad's mind.

"Seemed like a good sort."

Elena shot him a look.

"Dad."

"What?"

She kicked some sand, sending a squabble of gulls flapping in complaint.

"Your Gramps said they had a talk. About Grams."

"Jake had no business going there." Elena picked up a rock and hurled it into the sea.

"Actually, the way I understand it, it *is* his business." Gabe hugged her to his side. "He was only trying to help in the way he knows how."

"You really don't understand."

As small waves swirled around their feet, her father stopped and faced her. "I know a lot more than you think. As for your Grams, she has her reasons, but I don't agree with them anymore."

She nodded. "The world is different now."

"I respect my mother, Elena. She's been through a lot."

Elena shielded the sun with her hand. "What are you trying to tell me, Dad?"

"You have my permission to share whatever you think you need to with Jake. Don't let that old family story come between you two. That's long gone."

"But I promised Grams," Elena said, frowning. "I'll never break that promise as long as she's alive." She still felt guilty enough over sharing it with Allison all those years ago.

"I know, Honey promised, too." He looked skyward. "Just one warning. If you do tell him, don't let the press in L.A. get wind of it."

Agitated, Elena jammed her hands into the pockets of her sweatshirt. "It shouldn't matter to him."

"Probably won't, though it clearly matters to you. Call him."

Fuming at the thought, Elena started walking ahead, leaving her father behind.

"Elena."

Blowing out a breath in frustration, she whirled around. "You were the one who always told me not to call boys."

"Not Shane Wallace. That was a long time ago. I was right, too."

"Dad."

He caught up with her and took her hand in his.

For a moment, Elena felt like she was five years old, walking on the beach with her father, who'd always been her hero. Forever strong and always there. Yet, she'd almost lost him. On this trip, she'd learned how much she treasured her family. She blinked away sudden tears and flung her arms around him. "I don't ever want to leave you again."

He smiled. "Even little fairy-wrens grow up and leave the nest." Rubbing her back, he added, "I know you left your heart in L.A. I'd rather you go back and find it."

A few days later, early in the morning after saying goodbye to her parents and grandparents, Elena boarded her flight to Los Angeles and eased into her seat. This had been a heart-rending visit for her, from her father's brush with death to her affair with Jake. Following on the devastation of the robbery, she felt as though she'd been caught in an emotional cyclone, whirled from one disaster to another.

The wide-bodied airplane taxied the runway and lifted

off, gravity pressing her body weight into the seat, and then releasing its hold on her as the plane climbed through the sky. Relaxing in her seat, she scanned the perimeter of the Australian coast and watched it shrink in size until she could no longer see it.

She wished that her time with Jake could fade from her heart with the same ease.

Normally, she would have been more on guard against a man like Jake, except the shock of her father's illness and the robbery had combined to lower her defenses. Had he taken advantage of this, recognizing her vulnerability and need for comfort?

She bowed her head, realizing she'd been reckless, too.

Yet the sensation she'd felt for Jake had been like nothing she'd ever experienced before. It had seemed so real. Even now, she struggled against the tide of emotions inexorably drawing her back to him.

Resisting the feelings that continued to well within her, she turned her attention to a newspaper that a flight attendant had deposited on the empty seat next to her. She picked it up. *The Los Angeles Times.*

Flipping through it, a story headline caught her attention. "Jewelry Heist Costs Insurance Millions." She paused to read it. The article included an update on the investigation. The local police, along with the FBI's Los Angeles Division and the Major Theft Unit at FBI Headquarters, were working on the case. Investigators were following up on leads and urged the public to report any information, no matter how minor it might seem.

She read on. *Most jewelers were covered by insurance, with the exception of Elena Eaton, an independent jeweler who loaned jewelry reportedly worth millions to model Penelope Plessen, although value could not be confirmed. Neither Eaton nor Plessen could be reached for comment. While the detective work continues, with each passing day the likelihood of recovery diminishes.*

The article went on to discuss how insurance companies were working with investigators to determine actual losses.

Elena folded the newspaper and put it down. That was all she needed to know. After speaking with her grandmother, she'd accepted the fact that the jewelry's actual value could never be determined.

Without the major sale of the jewelry, she couldn't accomplish the dreams she'd planned, but she could still achieve her goals in other ways, though it would take longer. She sighed, recalling her plans.

Part of the profits would have gone to her parents to repay them for their loan to her. Another portion would have funded the expansion of her business through investment in inventory. A final share had been earmarked for charitable contributions in honor of her grandmother and her ancestors. The choice of how and where to spend it she'd entrusted to Lana, though Elena knew her grandmother's desire.

Those plans would have to wait.

Elena rested a pad of paper she'd brought on her lap, idly sketching new designs. Like her great-grandmother Sabeena, she'd forge on. That's all there was to do.

She didn't need Jake Greyson to swoop in and save her; she was fully capable of saving herself. Putting her head down, she went to work.

The next morning as the flight approached the runway at LAX, Elena closed her sketchpad and laptop computer. She'd slept little, having spent most of the trip sketching and planning a new line, as well as making a list of retail buyers to call on.

She could still capitalize on the media coverage Penelope had generated. Her cousin Poppy would be a huge help, and Elena knew she'd be thrilled to continue working with her.

Deep in thought, Elena tapped her nails on the in-flight tray in front of her.

If she could convince a luxury retail chain to take pieces on consignment to test the market to see how they sold, then she could promote the association. After this test marketing phase, if the store placed orders, then she could approach a bank for a working capital loan to cover production costs. It would be a slower growth process, but if she managed her inventory well, it could be successful.

However, it would probably be a long time before she could afford the materials she'd used in Penelope's suite of jewels. Unless she received custom orders, which could happen with the right publicity, she'd designed her last million dollar luxury pieces for a long, long time. Her future work would be luxury jewelry in more affordable ranges.

It had been a wild ride; however, she was thankful to have had the chance. For that, she was grateful to Sabeena for the risks she'd taken.

By the time the plane touched down on the runway, Elena had her future mapped out.

A future that did not include Jake Greyson.

19

Los Angeles, California

"SURPRISE," SAID ELENA as she stepped inside Fianna's busy shop. Upbeat music was playing, several stylishly dressed women were shopping and trying on outfits, and Fianna was in the midst of all the activity. Elena smiled. It felt good to return to old friends. Wanting to check on her shop, she'd come straight from the airport.

"Elena, you're back!" With her wild red curls flowing behind her, Fianna raced toward her and enveloped her in a hug. "I was so sorry to hear about your dad. How is he doing?"

"Much better. His prognosis is good."

"I've missed you so much," Fianna said, her voice rising with happiness.

"Have you been busy since I left?"

Fianna's eyes widened. "You have no idea. Once photos of Penelope wearing my dress began to circulate, I've had a hard time keeping up with sales." She nodded toward a couple of college-aged young women, who were creating a new fashion display with Fianna's spring fashion collection. "I have several interns from local colleges who want to learn the fashion trade. I don't know what I'd do without them."

"Love the new colors. So who are your new clients?" Elena was curious. They'd planned for a post-Academy Award rush for months, but neither of them knew if it would actually help their business.

"A lot of celebrities or their personal shoppers have called or come in," Fianna said. "The celebrity stylists want borrows, too." Her eyes sparkled. "Get this, a couple of boutiques want me to create trunk shows for them so women can order designs in their own size made to order."

"That's great for you. Really saves on the inventory cost." Elena inclined her head as a thought flashed through her mind.

Watching her, Fianna raised her eyebrows. "Are you thinking what I'm thinking?"

"We could coordinate shows with your fashion and my jewelry." Feeling excited, Elena spread out her hands in the air, mimicking a marquee. "Award-Worthy Hollywood Glamour."

"I'll introduce you to the buyers I've been working with," Fianna said. "This could be so much fun—and profitable."

Elena hugged her friend. "I spent the entire trip back

from Sydney revising my business and marketing plan. I hadn't thought of this, but it would be perfect. It solves my investment in inventory problem."

"Glad I can help. I've been so worried about you." Fianna moved a couple steps away from clients and lowered her voice. "Any news on capturing the thieves?"

"It's doubtful."

Fianna frowned. "Oh, I almost forgot. You had a couple of visitors while you were gone. Barbara Charles and the hot guy from the party."

"Jake." Elena ran a hand across the back of her neck, trying to remain calm. "That's her son, and he's an insurance investigator." She hesitated, not wanting to go into it, but Fianna was a close friend. Between Jake and her family, she'd been out of touch with her friends while she was in Sydney.

"I told them you'd left town. I had no idea when you'd return."

"It's okay. He came to Sydney to investigate the loss. Had some questions of me." She glanced away, flicking her fingernails. *The only way to get this out is to do it quickly.* "We went out a couple of times, but that's all over."

"*What?* You went out with him?"

"And it's over," Elena replied firmly. "All he wanted was information to help establish value on the jewelry."

Fianna frowned, looking puzzled. "You gave it to him, of course."

"As much as I could." Elena sighed. "Which wasn't

much."

Nudging her, Fianna asked, "So what happened?"

"He's just not my type," Elena said with exasperation, swinging her hair from her eyes. She knew Fianna doubted her, but there wasn't anything else she could say.

"I'm sorry," her friend said, resting her hand on her shoulder and rubbing her arm in commiseration. "You really liked him, huh?"

Elena could hardly reply. "Have to check on my shop," she said, backing away before she broke down and embarrassed herself in front of Fianna's customers. "See you later."

She hurried next door to her salon, jabbing the code on the security pad several times before she got it right. Locking the door behind her, she collapsed at her desk. *Damn him!* Why was he affecting her like this? She opened her mini-refrigerator and pulled out a water bottle.

She was guzzling water when she heard the front door buzzer. Ignoring it, she splashed water on her face, gasping to gain control and growing angrier at Jake for making her feel like this.

The doorbell buzzed again.

Someone was pretty insistent. She shook her head, chastising herself. She was here to work and make a living, not hide and cry in the back like a lovelorn teenager. This wasn't her first breakup. Sniffing, she stood up and smoothed her black knit dress.

Tapping sounded on the front glass. "Hello? Elena? I just saw you go in."

Who in the world? Wiping her eyes, she made her way to the front of her salon.

Elena pushed the heavy velvet drapery aside to reveal a perfectly coiffed blond woman dressed in a vivid orange dress. "Barbara Charles?"

The actress wiggled her fingers. "Welcome back. I've stopped by twice in the last few days. Fianna didn't know when you were returning, so I thought I'd take a chance."

Barbara made a turning motion with her hand, and Elena hurriedly unlocked the door for her.

"Just get in from Sydney?"

Elena nodded, trying to compose herself. "I came by here first to check on the shop."

Barbara peered at her. "Your eyes are quite red. That dry cabin air always affects me, too. Eye drops," she said, wagging her finger. "Don't ever travel without them. You never know who you'll meet. Years ago I had lunch with Coco Chanel at the Ritz in Paris. She told me, 'it's best to be as pretty as possible for destiny.'" She sank onto the blue velvet sofa and placed her Hermès purse next to her. "I met my fifth husband on a flight. So you see, Coco was right."

Barbara was looking at her expectantly. "May I get something for you? Tea, water, wine?"

"Champagne would be lovely. Or white wine, thank you." Barbara clasped her hands confidently and leaned forward to peer into the glass case. "You haven't put your jewelry out yet."

"Right away." Elena dashed to open a bottle of champagne she kept chilled in the refrigerator for guests. Glancing in the mirror above her desk, she almost cried out. No wonder Barbara suggested eye drops. She was a mess. Her hair was sticking up in all the wrong places. Hurriedly, she finger brushed her hair back and poured a glass for Barbara.

"Here are you," Elena said, delivering the champagne with a fresh smile that she didn't really feel. "I'll be back in a jiffy."

As Elena opened the safe in her office, she could hear Barbara take a phone call.

"Darling, how are you? No, I can't meet you. Why not?" She paused. "I'm at the most exquisite jewelry salon on Robertson—and *exclusive*. The jeweler just opened her doors for me. It's by appointment only, you know, and she's booked *weeks* in advance. I had to take Aimee Winterhaus to dinner and order practically the most expensive bottle of wine on the menu to get her appointment."

Elena's mouth fell open as she listened.

"Why, of course Aimee gave it to me, darling. I'm also Clover Lauren's godmother, aren't I, and every editor is clamoring to have the Grammy winner on her cover for holiday issues."

Smothering a laugh, Elena removed several velvet-lined jewelry trays and cradled them in her arms.

"Now darling, I must run. My appointment is starting and I can't be late." She paused. "Oh, didn't I say? Elena Eaton. The one who designed Penelope Plessen's jewelry for the Academy Awards. Yes, that one. Just wait until you see what she's making for me. *Ciao.*"

"And that's the way it's done," Barbara said with satisfaction as Elena entered. "You heard that, of course." She pointed to the door. "Keep that locked and put a sign on the door that says 'By Appointment Only.' The harder it is to buy from you, the more women in this town will clamor for you. Be a bigger snob than they are and they'll fling money at you."

Elena put the trays down on the glass case. "But I'm not the snobby type."

Barbara rested a finger on her chin. "No, I don't think you are. Well, play hard to get anyway. I know you can do *that*," she added pointedly.

Before Elena could think of anything to say that didn't involve her son, Barbara broke into a laugh. "I should be your publicist." And then, as if she'd just hit on a brilliant idea, she snapped a finger. "That's exactly what I'll do."

Elena opened her mouth to protest, but Barbara was faster.

"I'm not asking you to pay me, darling. I just enjoy helping talent when I see it. And I was the first to spot it, don't forget." She took a breath. "Now, I'm shopping for gifts today. Clover's birthday is coming up, and I think she absolutely *must* wear one of your pieces to a party soon, don't you?"

Listening to her, Elena's head was spinning. She wished she'd had another cup of coffee on the flight to keep up with Barbara. Surprisingly, she hadn't said a word about Jake. Surely he told her where he was going and why. But maybe he hadn't.

"She'd like this one." Elena held up a necklace designed after the one Penelope had worn. Fashioned in white gold, the lacy necklace was studded with small diamonds.

"That would do. But let's make it one of a kind. Clover loves emeralds, so can you add a few?"

Picking up her sketch pad, Elena deftly drew an idea she had. "How's this?"

Barbara nodded. "Very nice. You *are* talented."

Elena considered the drawing, then looked back at the necklaces she'd made. "I could customize these to make them exclusive."

"Now you're thinking."

Just then, Elena saw Fianna walk past her window and pantomime drinking a cup of coffee. Discreetly, Elena nodded. She was dying for a latte.

A moment later, Fianna backed up and peered in.

Elena picked up a pair of earrings to show Barbara. "Would you like earrings to match the necklace?"

Outside, Fianna slapped her hands on her cheeks in mock shock. It was all Elena could do to keep a straight face.

"What a good idea, yes."

"Then how about something like this to make them unique?" Elena sketched out a slight change.

Barbara's eyes sparked with delight. "I think Clover would love that. That will go with the most fabulous Versace mini-dress I bought her. And she has the legs, just like her godmother." Her eyes glistened with glee. "These would be perfect. Or *hot*, as you young people say."

By now, Fianna was gesturing wildly, and Elena was struggling not to laugh. Suddenly, Fianna's eyes widened and she hurried away.

Barbara glanced at the diamond watch she wore. "Oh dear, I must run. Call me with the price on that, and I'd like another one in a different design for me. Emeralds bring out my eyes, too," she said, rising.

"I will. Thank you, Barbara," she said, smiling. "And thank you for that call and your advice. That was quite a performance." Elena laughed softly as she opened the door for her.

"It was, wasn't it?" Smiling happily, Barbara tossed a scarf dramatically around her neck. Fluttering her fingers goodbye, she sailed out, her scarf floating behind her.

Watching her, Elena sucked in a sharp breath.

Jake was walking toward the shop. Barbara met him, and she motioned toward the salon.

Her heart pounding, Elena drew back behind the drapes, though she could still see them. "Damn it," she muttered to herself. "Hiding in my own shop." *Am I crazy?*

Elena stepped out from behind the drapes, pulled her shoulders back, and stood in full view. Defiantly, she folded her arms across her chest.

Jake's lips parted when he saw her, and he stumbled over the curb. Taking Barbara's arm, Jake turned away from Elena to lead his mother across the street.

Remaining rooted to her spot, willing herself to be strong, Elena almost jumped when her phone buzzed. It was Fianna.

Breathlessly, Fianna asked, "Did you *see* him?"

Channeling Barbara's coolness, she said, "I have no idea who you're talking about. But I do have an open bottle of champagne here."

"Be right there."

Elena sank onto the edge of the sofa and noticed her hands were shaking. Hating that her body was betraying her feelings, she remembered Barbara's words. *Play hard to get.*

No problem. How about impossible?

Because she wasn't playing his game ever again.

20

AFTER UNEXPECTEDLY SEEING Elena at her salon, Jake had spent weeks of restless nights thinking about her. The time they'd spent together in Sydney had been like a dream, though it had ended terribly. Once he'd stepped off the flight, he'd tried to compartmentalize his feelings like he'd always done.

Yet there was something about the sound of her laughter, her dancing blue eyes, the sexy little lotus flower tattoo on her neck…the feel of her arms around him, her lips on his mouth.

Only he couldn't seem to box up his feelings for Elena. Her memory seeped into his days and nights distracting him at the most inopportune moments.

Like now.

Cradling his phone on his shoulder, Jake swung around in his office chair until he was facing the window overlooking the palm trees lining Santa Monica Boulevard. He leaned back and propped his Italian leather shoe-clad feet on a low filing cabinet.

"Jake, you still there?" His lead investigator's voice barked through the line.

"Yeah. Sorry, can you repeat that last part?"

"Man, I don't know what's gotten into you since you got back from Sydney." The man went on to explain his most recent findings. "A tip came in from a young woman about a guy she'd dated. Seems she thinks he had something to do with the robbery. Something about money a pap paid him for photos."

"Does the guy have a name?" Jake grabbed a pad imprinted with Greyson Investigations, Incorporated and tapped his pen on it.

"Shane Wallace. He was on your list."

Jake narrowed his eyes as he listened.

"Tracked him down and tailed him for a while. Saw him trying to pawn a man's Piaget watch after he left General Carson's home in Brentwood. But there was no watch matching that description in the police records."

"Talk to him right away." Jake scribbled a note. "I saw him that night at the party." He didn't say that Shane used to date Elena. Nor could he imagine what Elena ever saw in the guy. They seemed ill-matched, but then, there was no accounting for some women's taste, and—

"Boss, you there? I think you keep cutting out. Can you

hear me?"

"Yeah, I'm here." *Hell, there I go again.* He threw down his pen and pushed his hand through his hair. He wished he could slice that woman out of his mind. "On second thought, I'll go see him."

His investigator tapped the phone. "Man, my phone has gone wonky. Thought you said you'd go—"

"I did. And I will."

There was a moment of silence on the line. "I thought you wanted me to handle the Elena Eaton follow-up."

"I do. Just not this guy. Address?" Jake scribbled a Culver City address on his pad.

"Boss?"

"Stop calling me that." He winced at himself. *Add irritable to the list.*

"Sorry. Jake, I've been trying to get Eaton to send me the receipts you wanted for materials—the platinum and anything else, like you said—but she won't respond. Want me to keep trying?"

"Yeah. Go by there."

"She's got a big 'By Appointment Only' sign on the door now. Doesn't answer."

Jake cursed under his breath. "Just. Keep. Trying." Why was she making it so hard for him to help her? He jabbed his phone off.

Call it intuition, but he'd always had the feeling Shane had something to do with the robbery. The police hadn't been able to find anything on the guy, except for petty incidents in the past. He seemed more interested in surfing and girls, and lately, older women with money.

As soon as he hung up, the phone rang again. Looking at the caller ID, he said, "Hi Mom, what's up?"

Impatiently, Barbara cleared her throat. "Haven't you forgotten something, darling?"

"No, why?"

"Our regular lunch date. You were supposed to be here nearly an hour ago. This isn't like you. Bad day at the office?"

"I completely forgot." He checked his watch and expelled a sigh. How had he missed this? "Be right there."

"You must be busy," she said breezily. "That's fine. I have a special project I'm working on and I'd be late for my flight if we were to keep our date now."

"Flight?"

"No time to talk about it now, darling. We'll talk after I return."

Frowning, he realized he'd definitely missed part of some conversation with her. Ever since she'd tried to drag him into Elena's salon with her, he'd been tuning out her efforts to push him into asking Elena out—and clearly some other details she'd shared. At least she'd finally given up on Elena. "Where are you going?"

"San Francisco. See you later, love you."

Frustrated, Jake stood and rested a palm on the wall by a window, thoughts of that last day with Elena crowding his mind again. Before he'd left Sydney, he'd told her he was through with her and her family since they wouldn't give him the information he needed to value the loss.

Yet he'd pushed through tough cases before. Why had he packed and left like a heartless machine even though she'd pleaded with him to stay?

The sound of the traffic below echoed the chaos in his brain. With Jenny, their relationship was safe and predictable; it was easily tucked away when he was busy. Effortless, almost. And dull.

Not so with Elena.

In truth, he'd been so irritated with her grandfather on their fishing trip that he'd stalked off the boat, exasperated in his attempt to help her, swearing off all of them. Why couldn't they just get out of the way and let him do his job?

Horns blared below as traffic snarled behind a fender bender, and he watched angry drivers shouting tirades in frustration at their inability to pass.

Slapping himself on the forehead, he realized impatience had fueled him, too. If he were honest with himself, his pride had been at stake. He'd built a reputation in this business of being the go-to guy to break difficult cases, and yet, he'd been unable to pry secrets from Elena and her family.

What an idiot he'd been. Those factors shouldn't have even entered into his relationship with Elena. How was he ever going to get through to her again to apologize?

And would she even let him?

Jake turned onto the street where Shane Wallace lived. He could have handed this information over to the police, and he would, but first he had some questions for Surfer Dude.

He figured that if Elena wouldn't have anything to do with him, the least he could do was try to help salvage her jewelry to show he cared.

Parking down the street, he started walking toward the address his investigator had given him. Small bungalows lined the tired lane, where old palm trees had grown so tall they looked leggy. Dodging palm fronds that had dropped onto the dried lawn and had been ignored, he approached Shane's door, listening.

Music blared from inside. Jake rapped his knuckles on the peeling wooden door. Taking a step back to peer through a window, he saw a shadow inside zip along a wall heading the other way.

After racing around to the back of the house, he lunged, grappling Shane and pinning him to the ground. "Going somewhere?"

"Hey, get off me." Taking in Jake's slacks and dress shirt, he blurted out, "You an undercover cop?"

"Nope. Private investigator. Hear you've been talking about the party at Bow-Tie."

Shane struggled, his blond hair matting in the dirt under him. "So what?"

"So you want to tell me, or tell the police?"

"Got nothing to say, mate." He spit in Jake's face.

Wiping his face with the back of his hand, he said evenly, "That's not what Mrs. Carson says. She could press charges, you know. Get you deported." *What a creep. What did Elena see in this guy?*

Shane's eyes widened. "How'd you know about Meredith?"

"I know a lot of things. Like you could go to jail for stealing her husband's Piaget."

Shane cursed. "What do you need?"

"The night of the party at Bow-Tie. You knew the thieves."

He strained against Jake's grip, but he was no match for him. Jake squeezed one of Shane's hands, nearly crushing it in his.

Thrashing in pain, Shane cried out. "Stop it!"

"Not until you tell me what you know."

"I didn't do anything."

Jake squeezed harder. *What a wimp.*

Writhing and kicking his bare feet against the dirt, Shane yelled. "The name's Gato."

Like the cat. Easing off the pressure, Jake said, "Gato what?"

Once Shane started talking, he spilled everything. Where he'd met Gato—Venice Beach—even the make and color of the car the guy drove.

Shane was practically crying. "He needed money, big money. He told me all he wanted was a chance to get in and take some photos he could sell to tabloids. So I told him how, helped him get in the back when no one was looking."

"He paid you?"

"A thousand bucks. I didn't know he was planning to rob the place. That's all I know, I swear, mate. You think I'd still be here if I were involved? I'm not!"

Jake sneered at him. "One more question. Elena Eaton."

"Miss Goodie Two Shoes? She had nothing to do with it." Shane blinked. "Felt kind of bad about her losing her stuff."

Jake had started to release him, but instead he tightened his grip. "Why? You still seeing her?" He had to go there, had to know.

"Hell no, she's my sister's best friend. Course I feel bad. I'm not heartless, you know."

"Your sister?" Furrowing his eyebrows, he asked, "Allison?"

"Yeah, she's my little sister."

"As in Allison and Zach?"

Shane's eyes widened. "Don't tell her you saw me. Shit, Zach hates me enough as it is."

Jake released him and stood, brushing dirt from his trousers. "Get out of here. And for God's sake, take that Piaget back to Mrs. Carson, you little—" He pushed his hand through the air to keep from punching some sense into

Shane.

Once Jake was back in his car, he made a call to a buddy of his on the police force. "Got a hot tip for you. Gato."

After he relayed the details Shane had told him, Jake turned his car toward Beverly Hills. By Appointment Only? He'd see about that.

21

San Francisco, California

"NOW, PUT YOUR hands together for the Collection in Bleue finale," Elena said to the crowd of stylish women who'd crowded into the store this morning for the Hollywood trunk show.

Amid the applause, Elena looked around, relieved and pleased now. After a rocky start where a necklace wasn't properly fastened and flew off when the model did a quick pirouette, the trunk show was now running smoothly.

With microphones in hand, Elena and Fianna perched on high stools in the women's salon of W.P. Harrison & Company, one of San Francisco's most fashionable stores just off Union Square. Attendees, dressed in the latest designer styles from Michael Kors, Dolce & Gabbana, and Vera Wang, sipped champagne mimosas and nibbled French pastries under glittering chandeliers. Models wearing Fianna's designs accessorized with Elena's jewelry circulated through the invitation-only gathering.

Dahlia sat to one side at a table that held exclusive perfumes she'd created to complement their designs. They had all worked together for weeks to create an immersive experience for attendees.

"Fianna really outdid herself with this glamorous vintage Hollywood look," Elena said as the model glided from the fitting rooms to an informal walkway over jewel-toned Persian rugs. "Fianna, why don't you tell us about your inspiration for this design?"

"Thanks, Elena," Fianna said, taking over. "This evening dress was inspired by azure waters, from the Malibu coastline to the Mediterranean and Sydney's Bondi Beach—all places the three of us love that have been significant in our lives."

Fianna went on to describe the closely fitted strapless dress that swirled around the model's legs. "Liquid blue silk lines a sheer white overlay studded with tiny icicles that reflect light and move with you. Look how lovely Tamara looks wearing this."

The model sashayed through the center of the room amid murmurs of approval. "And it wouldn't be complete without Elena Eaton Jewels," added Fianna.

Elena raised her microphone to take her turn as they'd rehearsed. "For this necklace, earrings, and bracelet set, I used diamonds with blue sapphires set in white gold. Inspired by the opulence of jewelry from India, it's a version similar to the cascading choker I designed for Penelope Plessen for the

Academy Awards." Despite having been nervous about speaking before the group, she lifted her chin with confidence, determined to overcome her fears and the wounds of the past.

"Also debuting today is Bleue Sparkle," Elena continued. "Dahlia Dubois designed this sensational new perfume to commemorate our Collection in Bleue." She held her hand out to Dahlia. "Be sure to try it and get an exclusive sample that's not available anywhere else in San Francisco."

Elena had just started selling the parfum in her salon, and she could hardly keep it in stock. Almost everyone who made a private jewelry appointment also left with a velvet-covered presentation box, in which one-ounce of the sensual floral parfum was nestled. She absolutely loved it.

Exchanging a smile with Dahlia, she went on. "Fittingly, Dahlia created Bleue Sparkle using a blend of blue flowers: lotus, iris, and delphinium."

The model posed and then executed a spin at the far end of the room while patrons broke out in applause. Before grasping Fianna's hand to thank the crowd and take a bow, Elena threw a grateful look at Barbara Charles, who looked resplendent in one of Fianna's royal blue dresses and Elena's sapphires.

Barbara had kept her word about helping Elena. Even better, over the past few weeks, Barbara had never mentioned a word about Jake. Elena could only assume he hadn't confided in his mother about their relationship in Sydney.

She'd rather have a friendship with his mother anyway.

Elena watched as salespeople approached private clients to answer questions and write orders. She and Fianna would stay to make design adjustments as needed. Elena loved helping women express their individuality to feel like the most beautiful versions of themselves.

"Ladies, you were fabulous," Barbara said to them, clasping their hands in each of hers. "And Dahlia, Camille's granddaughter. Why, I hadn't seen her since she was a child. Camille has always given the most elegant parties."

Elena laughed. *Is there anyone Barbara doesn't know?* "We really appreciate the introduction to W.P. Harrison." The boutique had been a mainstay of San Francisco style for decades. Elena studied the solidly accomplished crowd. "They have quite the client base."

"All the who's who in San Francisco." Barbara waved a hand laden with glittering stones across the room. "The opera ladies, high-tech women, theatre supporters—everyone is here. And what fun we had at dinner last night at Boulevard. I just love seeing old friends and meeting new people."

This was a different client segment than they had in Los Angeles—less glittery, more traditional, yet they were avidly placing orders.

Elena was so grateful to Barbara. They'd grown close over these last few weeks, and she'd developed strong respect for how talented and confident Barbara was and how well she'd managed her decades-long career. Working in

Hollywood wasn't for the faint of heart.

The four of them had flown to San Francisco yesterday to prepare for the trunk show this morning. True to her word, after Elena and Fianna had given trunk shows in San Diego and Orange County to Fianna's contacts at small shops, Barbara had announced that they were ready for an important client. She'd made calls to introduce them to the most exclusive boutique in San Francisco and arrange media coverage through her publicist.

Barbara had been delighted to give interviews about how she loved discovering talented young female designers and showcasing them. She even promised to match a percentage of sales with a donation from her charity to a local abused women's shelter and scholarships for women in the arts.

Fianna said, "How can we ever thank you enough?"

"Girls, I'm the one having fun," Barbara said. "At my age—which we won't discuss—juicy film parts don't come my way much anymore. I'm not one to sit idle." She embraced them before sailing away to meet another group of friends.

As Fianna watched Barbara work the room, she asked, "Does she ever say anything about Jake?"

"Not a word."

"Has he ever followed up on the insurance claim?"

Elena made a face. "He assigned one of his employees to the case." *Coward.* She shrugged. "He wants nothing to do with me. It's mutual." She was determined not to waste another minute of her life on him. However, that didn't stop him from invading her dreams completely unbidden.

"Such as waste." Fianna sighed. "He was awfully good-looking."

Elena shot her a withering look and changed the subject. "Are you ready for the weekend?"

Barbara had also asked them to put on a fashion show during the cocktail hour at a fundraiser for the National History Museum in Los Angeles, where a special exhibition, Diamonds of the World, was being presented in the museum's Gem and Mineral Hall. The event would raise funds for the Shelter Haven Home for abused women, where Elena had long volunteered. It was another charity Barbara supported, and with her, Elena had created a featured auction piece.

"I'll be ready, Fianna replied. "Thank goodness for my teams of interns and seamstresses. They're organizing and stitching as we speak. How's your new line going? Is it finished?"

"Barely. It's been crazy with my family coming, too." But that's exactly why Elena was pushing to get her new pieces completed. Since her father was now well enough to travel, her parents had decided to spend a month in San Diego with Honey's family, while her grandparents were going to a nearby yoga retreat.

Elena had a surprise planned for her family. Unveiling a special new design the night of the fundraiser was more perfect than she could have imagined. The new Sabeena design was named after her great-grandmother. Barbara had bought materials at cost for her, and the new jewelry would be auctioned to raise money for the charity.

Surveying with satisfaction the women placing orders, Elena dropped her voice. "Remember when we imagined our lives just like this?"

Fianna grinned. "We've worked a long time for this moment."

"You know I couldn't have done it without you." Elena had also relied on Fianna for moral support, especially while she was getting over Jake.

"We're stronger together."

"Always," Elena said, grateful for her friendships with women who'd become like sisters to her. Even those who had serious boyfriends still maintained their friendships. That was the mark of a true friend.

"I can't imagine the magnitude of what you've been through lately," Fianna said, shaking her head. "Every time I'd get overwhelmed with work, I'd think about you and how you've managed to survive such awful circumstances. After the robbery and your father's health crisis, I was worried you'd close up shop and return to Australia."

"I was tempted." She'd wanted to hide from Jake, too. Yet she also wanted to show him that she didn't need him or his help. This weekend would be proof of that. Although Barbara hadn't mentioned her son, Elena couldn't help but wonder if he'd escort her again as he had at the Academy Awards.

The next day after Elena returned home, she hurried to the airport to meet her family.

Bursting from the customs checkpoint at the international arrivals terminal, Honey threw her arms around her daughter. "Here we are," she said. "The Aussie Express is barreling through L.A."

Her father hugged her next. "How's my little fairy-wren?"

"Just great, Dad. Everything is really working out well now." They'd had a highly profitable day in San Francisco, and when she returned, a message from a buyer with a national luxury retailer was on her voice mail asking if she could meet with them in Dallas.

Her mother and father shared a look she couldn't quite understand, but then, the entire family was in high spirits. Her Grams and Gramps showered her with hugs and kisses, too. Chuckling over their antics, Elena led the rowdy group from the airport.

"Well, would you look at this," Gabe said, checking out the black SUV idling at the curb. "Wondered how you planned to pack us all in."

"This is Stefan, a friend of mine," Elena said. When she'd told Penelope over lunch one day that her family was arriving soon, her friend had suggested that Stefan bring the

SUV. "There's plenty of room, and Dad, don't you dare lift a bag." She couldn't believe how well her father looked after two months of rest, but his actions were still restricted.

"Welcome everyone, nice meeting you all." Stefan grinned and easily hoisted the suitcases, arranging them in the back while Elena directed her family.

"Dad in the front, Grams, you can sit in the middle with Mum, and I'll sit behind with Gramps." Elena was elated to see them all again and under such good circumstances. When she'd left Sydney, she'd been so despondent over Jake.

"We'll have a sensational time this weekend," Elena said, anxious to be on their way. "We have a big surprise in store for you." She beamed with happiness, imagining how much the new Sabeena design would mean to them.

Her mother and father traded swift glances. "She said 'we,'" Gabe said, chuckling. "That's my girl, Elena. I'm proud of you for coming back and going after what you wanted."

"Your soulmate," her mother said, tears of happiness rimming her eyes. "You and Jake. Your father was right."

Elena was appalled. Then she recalled what her father had said to her before she left Sydney... *I know you left your heart in L.A. I'd rather you go back and find it.*

Trying to recover, she said, "No Mum, we never saw each other again." She didn't count the Jake sighting outside of her shop.

"Elena, I'm...so sorry." Gabe stumbled over his words.

"I assumed you'd make up."

"He was so crazy about you," her grandmother said, pity etched on her face.

"Could've used some fishing pointers, though," Aaron added.

Elena spread out her hands, pushing air down in frustration while her eyes brimmed with angry tears. "Everyone *stop*. I don't want to hear anything about…*him*." She couldn't stand to even utter his name. Even after repressing her feelings for so long, she was shocked at how quickly the old pain surfaced again.

Her mother stroked her arm. "Not another word then. Shall we all go?"

Elena composed herself as Stefan drove to the boutique hotel that Elena had arranged for them in Beverly Hills. When they were nearly there, her grandmother leaned in.

"I have something very important to discuss with you, Elena."

Sensing an issue, the skin on the back of her neck tingled. "What is it?" Elena frowned. "Are you and Gramps, or Dad—"

"We're all fine and healthy, don't worry." Lana patted her arm. "I know you're busy with the upcoming event, but I'd like for you to make time for a talk today. Face to face. Stay while we check in."

Elena stiffened, wondering what Grams could possibly have to say.

After they arrived, Elena sat in the hotel garden waiting. A tiered fountain trickled, masking the coo of pigeons, while squirrels scurried along the top of the wrought iron fence surrounding the garden. The sweet, sun-warmed aroma of lavender and honeysuckle perfumed the air, but it did little to assuage the feeling of dread she had.

Her parents and grandparents arrived and joined her at the table. They seemed at ease, yet she couldn't shake the feeling that she was about to receive bad news.

"We wanted to discuss this with you as a family," her grandfather began. "Besides Lana, this concerns you most of all."

Her Grams clasped her hands on the garden table. "We've had a change of heart because we've seen how the promise you made affected you when you visited us in Sydney." Her grandmother's deep mahogany were fixed on her.

"Now more than ever," Honey added. "Based on what you told us about…"

Knowing her mother was referring to Jake, Elena shot her a warning look. Her skin crawled with unease.

"I would never divulge our secret, Grams." Elena still felt guilty for her teenage mishap, but she hadn't caved when Jake had pressed her. "Except for that one time."

"No harm done." Honey patted her shoulder. "Just listen."

With a faraway look in her eyes, her grandmother reeled

back in time. "My mother was born nearly a hundred years ago into a very different world. As you know, she escaped cruel circumstances and a disastrous situation, further risking her life in her journey to Australia. Had she stayed in India, Sabeena would surely have been killed."

Lana paused to look at the faces around the table. "With the exception of my husband and Honey, we would not be here today. Not me, not my son, nor you, Elena. That is the simple fact."

Elena nodded with deep respect. Sabeena's courage had given her life.

"Today, my mother is at rest and beyond worldly prosecution," Lana said. "Yes, she killed a man. Yes, she entered the country illegally, smuggled in the dead of night by her benefactor, Aaron's mother. And yes, unjustly accused of theft." Lana squeezed her husband's hand. "As you know, we lived with an underlying fear for many years."

"Grams, I understand why it's important." Though Lana rarely spoke of her early life before Sydney, Elena knew it had been painful for her. She would do anything to protect her grandmother. "I will never divulge your secret."

"Oh no, dear. My priorities have changed." Lana shook her head, her white hair gleaming in the sunlight. "I am beyond caring what the world thinks of me now. And I want you to be completely free of this burden, too." She clasped Elena's hands. "It's time for Sabeena's story to be told."

Elena sat back, surprised.

"And I want you to tell it."

"Me?" The thought of doing this went counter to all she'd been instructed to do in her life. Uncertainty clouded her mind.

Her grandmother regarded her carefully. "It's your story, too. The success you're having is also Sabeena's success. She risked her life to transport the colored stones that others shunned."

22

"ABSOLUTELY EXCEPTIONAL." ELENA tilted her head to gaze up at an astounding, larger-than-life bronze statue depicting a trio of draped goddesses. Each goddess helped support a glowing amber, electrically lit globe in their uplifted hands. The masterpiece stood in the center of a soaring rotunda at the Natural History Museum near downtown Los Angeles.

"This is called the *Three Muses*," Barbara said, pride evident in her voice. "One of my favorites, it was installed in 1913. The goddesses represent History, Science, and Art. The sculpture was created by Julia Bracken Wendt, who rose from domestic servitude to become the foremost sculpturist in the West in her time."

"We stand on the shoulders of our ancestors," Elena said, remembering a quote and thinking of her great-grandmother as she stood in awe of the artistry.

It was after museum hours, so the charity had reserved the venue for the evening. Classical music echoed through the cavernous structure, and a profusion of floral arrangements created a festive environment.

Patrons in evening wear were filtering into the rotunda, their heels tapping on mosaic tiles, their laughter bouncing off Italian marble walls. From here they would spill into the Gem and Mineral Hall for the private exhibition, Diamonds of the World.

"People have already been admiring your jewelry." Barbara touched the necklace she wore with reverence. "I'm sure the Sabeena Suite will fetch a fine price in the auction. The charity will be so grateful."

"I'm so pleased you gave me this opportunity." Elena kissed her on the check.

Barbara bloomed with happiness at her gesture. "You're like a daughter to me, darling."

"I only hope that someday when I find a man to love, he has a mother with your spirit." Thankfully, no mention of Jake had been made. Elena hadn't seen him, and didn't want to ask his mother if he would be here. The less said, the better. She would certainly keep her distance if he appeared.

Elena stepped back to admire her work on Barbara.

The actress looked resplendent in a draped, goddess-style chiffon dress Fianna had designed. In white, it was a perfect showcase for the necklace from Elena's latest collection. She'd used an array of blue gemstones, including sapphire and tanzanite for the bracelet, earrings, and necklace. At the center of the lacy, Indian-inspired cascading choker necklace was a rare blue diamond, one of the last of Sabeena's stones. The Sabeena Suite would be auctioned at the end of the evening. This time, a bodyguard shadowed Barbara and the museum had stepped up security for the exhibit.

"There you are," Honey called out.

Elena's parents and grandparents arrived together. Because Elena had to set up with Fianna and prepare the models, they had arrived earlier to work and changed at the museum.

After introducing Barbara to her family, Elena gestured to her jewelry, resting her fingers on the sparkling necklace. "Here's my surprise this evening. Introducing the Sabeena Suite. The necklace is the crown jewel of my Bleue Collection."

"How exquisite." Lana's eyes sparkled with emotion as she admired it. "Your work has truly transcended the ordinary, dear."

"Is there significance to the name?" Barbara asked.

Elena nodded toward her grandmother. "Grams, why don't you tell her?"

"Sabeena was my mother's name," Lana said. "It's an Indian name, and it means 'beautiful.' As she truly was. Beautiful and strong."

Lana drew her hands across Elena's face. "My beautiful granddaughter. Sabeena would have been so proud of you."

"Then I believe this is rightly yours to wear tonight."

Reaching up, Barbara removed the necklace and fastened it around Lana's neck.

"Oh, Grams, it's gorgeous on you." Seeing her grandmother wearing the creation that meant so much to both of them unleashed an unexpected wellspring of emotion in Elena. She turned to Barbara. "That's so kind of you."

The jewelry was stunning against the shimmering fabric Lana wore. Fianna had encouraged both Lana and Elena to wear sapphire gowns from her Bleue Collection tonight.

Elena helped the two women exchange jewelry, then Barbara looped her arm with Lana's.

Glancing at Honey, Gabe, and Aaron, Barbara said, "Would you all like to see the big rocks?"

"It's a spectacular exhibit," Elena said. She had toured it earlier because she knew that she'd hardly have a chance to view it tonight. "You'll see the Argyle Violet Diamond from Australia, as well as the thirty-carat Juliet Pink Diamond. It's set in a necklace with nearly a hundred carats of diamonds. And there's a rare purple diamond, the Victorian Orchid."

Aaron chuckled. "You mean we flew twelve thousand kilometers to see rocks from our own backyard?"

Honey playfully swatted her father-in-law. "Come on, let's go and leave Elena to her work." To Elena she added, "It's so exciting to see you in action."

"Don't forget to see the regular collection, too," Elena said. "The blue Benitoite has an unusual crystal formation, and the Elbaite tourmaline is a one of the world's finest large examples."

After they all left, Elena returned her attention to the event. She'd asked Poppy to oversee a display of her work that Barbara had insisted be included. She wiggled her fingers in a wave to Poppy, who smiled with excitement. "How's it going?"

"I've been giving out your card a lot. I also booked two appointments for you," Poppy added with a little squeal. With her shimmering blond hair, she was surrounded by young men in smart tuxedos who seemed more admiring of her than the jewelry, yet she was still tending to business, making sure the jewelry matched the outfits and was accounted for while the models changed. A museum guard stood nearby.

Elena scanned the appointments and cards Poppy had collected. "I don't know what I would've done without your help these last few months."

Next to Poppy, Fianna was speaking with two of her interns, who were busy overseeing the ongoing fashion show. "I might hire Poppy myself," Fianna said.

"I'll keep that in mind," Poppy said. "I'm out of school soon."

Models wearing the Bleue Collection were slowly circulating among guests in the rotunda and beyond in the dinosaur room. The classical musicians increased their volume as the conversation elevated.

Soon it would be time to begin the dinner and auction.

Tables had been set outdoors on an adjoining patio under clear, balmy skies. Elena blew out a breath to calm her nerves and turned around to mingle with guests.

"Elena."

She'd turned right into Jake, who was so close she could feel his breath when he uttered her name. Averting her eyes from his gaze, she pressed her fingertips back against his chest and fought to maintain her composure. "Your mother is—"

"I'm not looking for her. I came to see you."

She raised her gaze, meeting his. "What's the use, Jake? It's over."

"Those days in Sydney...something special happened, something I've never felt before in my life. I know you felt it, too." He searched her eyes. "We have a connection, Elena. Can you deny it?"

Biting her lip, she tried to turn away but he stopped her with a simple touch of his hand to hers. The old fire erupted between them, capturing her in her place.

Fighting against it, she took a step back. "We don't share the same values. What's important to you, isn't to me."

"I was, as your father would say, a complete *arse*." Jake trailed a finger on her arm. "I was wrong to pressure you—and your family—to divulge information you didn't want to. That shouldn't have mattered as it did to me. You are more important than any of that."

Elena shook her head as if she could shake the hold he had over her from her mind. "It doesn't matter anymore."

"Believe me, I only had what I thought was your best interest at heart," Jake said, his voice carrying a sense of urgency.

"That's not the way I remember it." Elena turned from him to flee, but he caught her hand. The warmth and strength of his grip radiated through her, stilling her feet.

"Please, listen. You and your family taught me what's really important. I know now it's not about the money, or even catching the bad guys. It's about trusting those you love. I had to learn that the hard way, but I promise I'll never forget it."

Elena fluttered her eyes closed, unable to face him. *Why couldn't he have had this epiphany when we were in Sydney?* She'd suffered so much, but he sounded like he had, too. Opening her eyes, she asked, "Why did you run away when we'd just had the most incredible beginning?"

Sighing, Jake clasped her hand to his chest. "I was a frustrated and prideful idiot. I've never felt about anyone the way I feel about you, and I didn't know how to give my feelings—and yours—the priority we deserved."

"Leaving so suddenly like that, especially right after…" Recalling her anguish, she pressed her fingers against her throbbing temple. "That was demeaning. It hurt."

Moving closer, Jake smoothed his hand over her cheek, stopping to brush a tear away. "I'm so sorry," he whispered. "Never again."

She gulped against the emotion that threatened to

overtake her. "I should tell you about Grams…and her mother."

"You don't need to. I only care about you." He wrapped his arms around her.

Elena nearly cried out at the feel of his embrace as memories of their lovemaking in Sydney flooded her mind. How could she be so weak?

"I know what's important now," he said, tipping her chin. "I promise I won't let you down again. Can you be brave enough to give me another chance?"

Elena gazed into velvety brown eyes that shone with the same adoration she'd seen in Sydney. "Loving another person takes strength."

"We're stronger together," he said, lowering his lips to hers before he paused.

Closing her eyes, she summoned the courage to meet his lips, promising herself to trust him, and her own feelings, too.

They kissed deeply, and then she felt Jake smiling against her lips, and she responded by flicking her tongue, teasing him.

Clasping her hand to his chest, he swayed slightly to the music.

A mixture of relief and happiness surged within her, and she responded, swaying on her toes and smiling up at him.

Impetuously clutching her, Jake swirled her in a happy, impromptu dance around the *Three Muses*, an expression of pure love filling his face. Bystanders began clapping at their spontaneity.

Elena threw her head back, joyously laughing with him while she released all the animosity and sadness that had gripped her heart.

Other couples began dancing around the statue with them, and soon the entire atmosphere in the rotunda was one of pure delight.

Later that evening at dinner, Elena and her family joined Barbara at her table. Sitting next to Jake, she held his hand under the dark blue table cloth, anxiously awaiting the auction.

When Barbara and Honey had appeared in the rotunda entry and saw her and Jake dancing, the two women had hugged each other with happiness, and Barbara quickly changed the seating arrangements at two tables so they could all sit together. "Thank goodness I don't have to separate you two anymore."

Kissing Elena's hand in his, Jake said, "I thought you were doing quite the opposite, Mom."

Barbara smiled coyly. "I knew you'd find your way back to each other. Just took longer than I expected."

Elena looked around the table counting those she loved. Her parents and grandparents, Barbara, Fianna, Poppy, and Dahlia. Seeing their faces gave her the strength to do what she planned this evening.

They listened to the president of the Shelter Haven

Home organization discuss the need for acquiring another location and providing counseling to families suffering from physical domestic violence and mental abuse. The president thanked the patrons for donating generously, and then the auction commenced for vacation trips and celebrity memorabilia.

Finally, Elena heard her name announced. The Sabeena Suite was expected to draw the highest bidders.

Jake squeezed her hand and kissed her cheek. "Go do good," he said, grinning. "Make them pay for your brilliance."

Gathering her courage, she made her way to the podium, followed by Lana and Barbara. Glancing back, she saw her family and friends clapping loudly, urging her on.

With her grandmother and Barbara standing beside her, united in their cause, Elena leaned into the microphone.

"I'm here tonight, not only to auction a lovely piece of jewelry that my grandmother is wearing, but also to share a personal story that demonstrates the impact that domestic violence can have on a family throughout the generations."

The audience quieted. Elena stared out among them, finding Jake, and growing calmer as she discovered a reservoir of strength within her. "This story isn't about jewelry or money. This is a story of abuse and repression and what one woman was forced to do to reclaim her life and her sanity. And what she did to protect and provide for her child. Her name was Sabeena." She turned to her Grams. "And she was the mother of my grandmother, Lana."

Her head held high, Lana nodded to her to continue.

"My great-grandmother Sabeena was born near Golconda, India in the early nineteen-hundreds," Elena said. "She went from being the daughter of a Maharajah—a princess—to being the wife of a rich but cruel man. Even though he was a man of stature and his family received a high dowry, he was relentless in his abuse, both physical and mental."

Elena went on. "One night, Sabeena fought back to save herself from certain death. She barely prevailed, yet she never meant to take a life. Had she not fled, her husband's family would have surely killed her, even though it was self-defense and she bore many scars to prove it."

Glancing at her grandmother, who smiled with encouragement, Elena continued. "Recovering from her injuries, Sabeena was smuggled into a new country by a kind woman who understood her plight, but there she was looked down upon because of her skin color. It wasn't long before she was taken advantage of again because she could not fight back hard enough."

She pressed her lips together. "Yet, Sabeena did not give up. She gave birth to a daughter and fought her entire life. Fought for her life, fought against humiliation, fought for a better life for her daughter—my Grams. So I vowed to continue the fight for her and others like her."

Elena paused to blink back tears. She couldn't imagine

enduring what her great-grandmother had. Lana turned to embrace her. This was a moment of healing for her entire family, as important for her as it was for her grandmother.

"Will you say a few words, Grams?"

Trading places with her, Lana looked out over the audience. "As a girl, my mother—and her mother before her—had collected alluvial stones scattered along ancient river beds that others thought useless because of their color. Flawless white diamonds had the highest value, and only the elite were allowed to wear and display these. The lower castes were allowed other less valuable colors. Unless a colored stone was the size of an egg, it had little value, particularly if it were flawed with even the most minor inclusions."

Elena could see her father and grandfather beaming with pride at the step Lana had taken.

"Sabeena had rare blue eyes—like my granddaughter—so she collected and traded stones with other girls until she had a collection of rough blue diamonds. When she escaped, she traveled with her stones and some jewelry sewn into her clothing and a doll she'd had as a girl, the only items she took from her homeland."

Lana touched the necklace she wore. "Sabeena left most of her beautiful jewelry with her husband's family, taking only what she could carry that her mother had given her. To survive, she sold off her fine jewelry for food and for my education, yet those little stones—her touchstones with her past—helped her to keep going."

Turning to Elena, she said, "My granddaughter used most of Sabeena's remaining diamonds to create a one-of-a-kind jewelry suite for Penelope Plessen to wear at the Academy Awards in homage to Sabeena. As most of you know, that was stolen. But that didn't stop Elena. Tonight, we will auction the jewelry I'm wearing, which has one of Sabeena's last remaining blue diamonds. The rest of the gemstones and materials were donated by Barbara Charles."

Applause thundered across the crowd. Elena gazed out at Jake, who was standing and clapping along with the rest of her family and friends.

Elena hugged her grandmother, knowing the strength it had taken for her to share her story. Speaking into the microphone, she said, "When you wear this necklace, you will be honoring Sabeena, a survivor, whose name means 'beautiful.' All proceeds will go to help others become triumphant, beautiful survivors, too."

Next to her, Barbara was smiling radiantly. Slipping past, Barbara assumed her place comfortably in front of the microphone. "How about some opening bids?" she asked, teasing the audience with her famous, seductive voice. She named a dollar amount, and within seconds, bidding commenced.

Lana stepped from the stage to circulate among the patrons, letting them get a closer look at the jewelry.

Elena couldn't have been more proud of her grandmother. And of Barbara, who was in her element, egging on wealthy members of the crowd to be generous with their support in the vigorous bidding war. "Won't this be a stunning part of your fall opera ensemble?" she said, directing her comment to women in the audience. "Or wear it with nothing but a negligee, darling."

Meeting Jake's eyes, she saw such pride and encouragement reflected there, too. Their story, like Sabeena's, had also come full circle tonight. Elena smiled, her eyes brimming with happiness.

The bids climbed higher until finally Barbara brought down the gavel with a resounding thud. "Sold!" she cried. People sprang to their feet, clapping and congratulating the generous bidder. A Beverly Hills couple from Mumbai who'd founded a biotech company together were the victorious new owners. Elena was so pleased they'd bought it; she knew the woman from her volunteer work.

After posing for photos, Lana delivered the jewelry to the purchasers, who deeply appreciated its history, and were also dedicated to helping curb domestic violence. Elena and Barbara stood with them for more photos before leaving the podium.

Elena was making her way through the skirted tables when Jake met her halfway. Cradling her face in his hands, he said, "You were amazing. And your grandmother. What an honor to be with such incredible women tonight." Looking embarrassed, he added, "Now I feel ashamed for trying to wrangle such a sensitive secret from you and your family."

"Shh," Elena said, pressing her finger against his lips. "That's all in the past." Taking his hand, she guided him back to their table.

Later over coffee and dessert, Elena was chatting with her grandparents at the table when Jake leaned over.

"May I cut in?" he asked. "I owe Aaron and Lana an apology for my thoughtless behavior in Sydney."

"You didn't know, son," Aaron said, putting his arm around his wife. "But we appreciate the thought now. Lana went through a lot in her life."

"It was complicated," Lana said. "But my mother was my rock. To a great extent, she lived through me. She lived in fear of deportation, which would have meant a certain death sentence. There in India, she was called a murderer and a thief, and was an embarrassment to her family. But in dreaming for me, she found freedom."

Elena slid a hand over hers.

"We created new identities," Lana said. "Only Aaron knew my true heritage. It was also a time in history when we were not readily accepted in the society where we lived. Non-white immigration to Australia was severely restricted until the early nineteen-seventies." She took her husband's hand. "Aaron and I grew up together, my mother worked in his mother's home as her personal maid, even though they weren't wealthy."

"Actually, they became the closest of friends," Aaron

said. "Sabeena was like family to me. My mum was a good soul from Yorkshire. Out to settle a new world and help others."

"There's more to the story, too." Elena turned to Jake. "One of Lana's distant cousins in India became an attorney. She'd grown up hearing about the woman who'd disgraced the family long ago, but she'd always had questions, so last year she decided to investigate. Based on witness statements and police and medical records, she determined that Sabeena had acted in self-defense."

Elena paused, touching one of Sabeena's blue diamonds she wore at her neck. "From old letters and photos taken before her marriage, our cousin confirmed what we always knew—that the jewelry and diamonds Sabeena had been accused of stealing were actually her *stridhan*, her personal property protected by law to do with as she pleased."

Smiling, Elena clasped her grandmother's hand. "Thanks to our cousin, Sabeena was recently found innocent of all accusations under the law and completely absolved."

"That's quite a story," Jake said. "Now I understand your reticence to share it."

As the band played and the music filled the air, Lana looked around the table. "Now you all know the story. Enough of history. It's time for the living." Throwing a swift look at Elena and Jake, she took her husband's hand. "It's time to show those two they're not the only ones who know how to dance."

While everyone at the table emptied onto the dance floor, Elena and Jake stayed seated.

"I'm in no hurry," Elena said, wanting to spend time alone with Jake. She felt a slow burn of desire for him building within her again.

"I hope we have the rest of our lives to dance." His dark eyes sparkled with longing. "Look at your grandparents." Caressing her cheek, he said, "I'm not surprised you're descended from an Indian princess. And I thought Allison was kidding."

"I wanted to throttle her that night," she said, though now it no longer mattered. She was proud of who she and her family were. She always had been.

"Ah, but what a memorable night it was, and one I can't wait to repeat. Without the hailstorm, that is." Reaching out, Jake touched the tiny, blazing blue diamond that sparkled on her nose. "I've always thought that was adorably sexy. One of Sabeena's?"

"To remember her by," she replied. "She once told Grams she considered these lucky stones." Elena smiled, convinced of it now. "I think this proves it." Then, twining her fingers with his, she pulled him to his feet. "We need a new adventure."

"I'm game," he said, waggling his eyebrows. "What do you have in mind?"

"Let's explore." Leaving the crowd behind, she led him back into the museum, where they strolled into the rotunda.

They could still hear the music outside.

Swaying her hips, Elena felt the rhythm move in her. "About that dance…"

Sweeping her once again into his arms, Jake waltzed with her around the *Three Muses*, laughing and stealing kisses. Most everyone else was outside, so they had the place to themselves, except for a few stragglers and security guards.

Their feet tapping on the tile, they danced into the dinosaur room, sailing around Thomas the Tyrannosaurus Rex and the Triceratops, which were safely cordoned off.

Security guards were laughing and clapping along with them, catching the exuberance of their contagious *joie de vivre*.

Elena tipped her head back and laughed as Jake spun her through the front doors of the museum, the effervescence of their love bubbling over into the cool night air.

Outside, at the top of the long, wide concrete steps that led down into a rose garden, Jake whooped and jumped onto a bannister, sliding down on one hip while Elena raced breathlessly beside him.

At the end of the steps, she fell into his arms, both of them laughing hysterically as they joined hands and continued dancing through rows of roses, which were releasing heavenly perfume into the evening air.

All at once, Jake's phone buzzed in his pocket.

"You're not answering that," Elena said, playfully snatching it from his tuxedo pocket and stretching her arm away from him.

As he reached for the phone, she tried to turn it off but accidentally connected the call.

"Hello, Jake? You there?"

Slapping her hand over her mouth, Elena tried to suppress a giggle.

Jake grabbed the phone from her, attempting composure. "Jake here, but it's really not a good time." He started to hang up, but then listened for a moment, a smile growing on his face.

"What? What?" Elena repeated, leaning in to hear the conversation.

Suddenly, Jake thrust his fist into the air in jubilation. "Yes! Yes, yes, yes!" He disconnected the call and flung his arms around Elena, lifting her from the path and swirling her around.

"Tell me!" she cried, pounding his chest.

Swinging to a stop, Jake clutched her to him. "They found your jewelry."

Elena let out a scream of joy and jumped into Jake's arms, pulling his full mouth to hers.

"Where?"

Jake shook his head. "A French customs agent found the jewelry in the base of a large Miss Piggy statuette imported into France by a collector."

Laughing, Elena said, "Well, she always did like diamonds."

As they celebrated everything that night—family, forgiveness, love, and the rarest of blue diamonds—Elena thought Jake's kisses had never tasted so sweet.

And she knew the best was yet to come.

- The End –

Wondering what's next?
You've met Honey Bay Eaton. Next meet the rest of the fun-loving Bay family of Southern California in Jan's next series.

Sign up now to hear about this new release.
Join Jan's mailing list (and get a free read!)

Other Books by Jan Moran

Contemporary
The Love, California Series:

Flawless

Beauty Mark

Runway

Essence

Style

Sparkle

20th Century Historical
The Winemakers: A Novel of Wine and Secrets

Scent of Triumph: A Novel of Perfume and Passion

Life is a Cabernet: A Companion Wine Novella to The Winemakers

Nonfiction
Vintage Perfumes

About the Author

Jan Moran is a writer living in southern California. A few of her favorite things include a fine cup of coffee, dark chocolate, fresh flowers, laughter, and music that touches her soul. She loves to travel just about anywhere, though her favorite places for inspiration are those rich with history and mystery and set against snowy mountains, palm-treed beaches, or sparkly city lights. Jan is originally from Austin, Texas, and a trace of a drawl still survives to this day, although she has lived in California for years.

Her books are available as audiobooks, and her historical fiction has been widely translated into German, Italian, Polish, Turkish, Russian, and Lithuanian, among other languages.

Jan has been featured in and written for many prestigious media outlets, including *CNN, Wall Street Journal, Women's Wear Daily, Allure, InStyle, O Magazine, Cosmopolitan, Elle*, and *Costco Connection*, and has spoken before numerous groups about writing and entrepreneurship, including San Diego State University, Fashion Group

International, The Fragrance Foundation, and The American Society of Perfumers.

She is a graduate of the Harvard Business School, the University of Texas at Austin, and the UCLA Writers Program.

Visit Jan at JanMoran.com. If you enjoyed this book, please consider leaving a brief review online for your fellow readers where you purchased this book, or on Goodreads. Authors appreciate reviews. Thank you!

Lightning Source UK Ltd.
Milton Keynes UK
UKHW010132200422
401743UK00002B/440

9 781942 073932